Fall Awakening

Southern Blue Blood, Volume 1

Serenity Snow

Published by Serenity Snow, 2023.

FALL AWAKENING

First edition. January 31, 2023.

ISBN: 979-8224309535

Written by Serenity Snow.

Table of Contents

Prologue

Ryan had to hide a smile as the woman in front of her averted her gaze. Amelia Rose-Brier was stunning with her strawberries and cream skin and copper red hair pouring over her small shoulders.

She was delicate boned but not thin. She had a curvy body that had evoked more than one night of illicit dreams since Ryan had met her a few weeks ago.

"So, you decided to venture out with Miss Genny to pick up a few treats from the Farmer's Market," Ryan commented, and Amelia looked at her again, her green eyes the color of jade.

Amelia nodded. "I wanted to get some cherries and peaches."

"You know, the best peaches I ever had, came from a small orchard not too far from here. They grow the most delicious cherries and strawberries ever too. They hothouse grow the berries in the winter, but they are still great."

"Really?" Amelia asked and those pretty eyes lit up.

"I'll show you," Ryan said. "So, how've you been? I haven't seen you in the restaurant for a few days."

Amelia's face was a mask of surprise now. "I wasn't feeling well," she said. "I think I got too much sun."

"Red, you really should wear a hat to cover that pretty skin in summer."

"I know," she said. "I don't know what happened. I normally do, but I forgot it. I was out with a couple of the girls from the inn."

Ryan nodded. "So, you're better now?"

Amelia smiled, showing genuine pleasure that someone cared. "Yes. Thank you."

"Good to hear," Ryan murmured. "Why don't you just get your fruit from the inn's kitchen?"

"We don't have a lot of peaches, so I leave them for cooking and for the guests."

"Makes sense," Ryan commented. "So, cherries? A favorite treat for you?"

"I love them, yes. What about you?"

"I've had my share." She gave Amelia a wink. "Some are sweet. Some are tart. Which one are you?"

Amelia gave her an uncertain look and colored.

Ryan chuckled. "Here we are," she said.

"Hey, Ryan," one of the women at the stand drawled. "Come by for some peaches?"

"I believe I might have three or four," she said. "Amelia, this is Bobbi-Sue. Her family runs Old Brier Farms where this fruit comes from."

"Oh. Hi." Amelia's voice was a little cool, but Ryan had come to realize that she wasn't cold at all, just shy and uncertain.

"Hi, Amelia," Bobbi-Sue replied and then turned an angry gaze on Ryan. "Are you kidding me?" She dropped a hand on her hip, her gray eyes growing stormy.

Ryan shrugged. Bobbi-Sue had been trying to get in her pants again for months now. She hadn't bought Ryan's no was as simple as she wasn't into casual sex anymore. Bobby-Sue wasn't looking for a wife just Miss Right Now.

"Right. I knew it wasn't that simple."

Ryan snorted. "Baby, I say what I mean and mean what I say when it comes to most things."

"Sure, whatever. Amelia, what can I get you, honey?"

"Um, a half-pound of cherries, same of strawberries and four peaches."

Bobbi-Sue smiled. "You'll never buy another peach from the store after you've had ours. My daddy knows peaches and cherries."

"I'm looking forward to trying them," Amelia said.

Bobbi-Sue got Amelia's order packaged, and Amelia paid. "Enjoy, Amelia, and come back, ya hear." Bobbi-Sue gave her a big smile.

"Thanks."

"Amelia. Come over here."

"Thanks, Ryan. Thank you, Bobbi-Sue." Amelia slipped her bag into the canvas bag on her shoulder.

"You know, Amelia, there's a booth called Nan's. Check it out. Nan brings some of her best lingerie out here." She winked. "Ryan will love you in it."

"Yeah, I would," Ryan agreed giving Amelia a wink, and she colored.

"Excuse me," Amelia mumbled and hurried over to Hope, one of her co-workers from the inn.

"Got your peaches all bagged. I can't believe you're fooling around with that ice queen. She's not even your type. I bet she makes you wish she was me," Bobbi-Sue said keeping her voice low.

Ryan grunted and pulled out her wallet. She gave Bobbi-Sue a bill. Keep the change and pick up a clue." Ryan walked away shaking her head. The woman thought she was the shit, but she could do without her brand of sweetness.

Bobbi-Sue couldn't keep her panties up, when she wore any. She was willing to spread her legs for any woman willing to go down on her. She was also a big fan of menages or multiple partners at once. Not Ryan's cup of tea. On top of that, Bobbi-Sue preferred women with money to spend on her.

She wasn't all about going broke over a piece of tail that couldn't keep her legs together. But now Amelia—Her gaze wandered to the retreating form with the gentle swaying hips.

Damn she had a great ass.

"Ryan Baptist," Genevieve Honeywell said her name in a chiding tone, and Ryan jerked her gaze from Amelia's very shapely ass.

It was only 9, and the August morning was sunny and H.O.T. Most people arrived at the market as soon as it opened to get a jump on the heat and the crowd.

"Ma'am," Ryan answered turning her gaze on the older woman. Miss Genny Honeywell came bustling over with a bag in hand.

"I've been trying to get in touch with you," she said. "I really need a favor."

"Oh?" Ryan asked with a frown. What could the woman possibly need from her? Miss Genny was rumored to be one of the most successful and wealthy business owners in town.

She owned an inn that seemed to be doing well, despite the damage the pandemic had done to some businesses in the hospitality industry.

She was also owner of Avon Del Park with its natural beauty and expanse. Entrance into the park was free, but there were tour packages as well as event packages and a small trailer area where campers could park a trailer for a night, a week or put down stakes for longer.

That came with a cost especially since there were hookups for running water, propane tank rentals, and a lounge for cooking that boasted two small kitchens with dining areas. There was also Wi-Fi access.

"Can you come over tomorrow? I need to discuss business with you."

"What kind of business?" Ryan worked in investments at the local bank, but she was an MBA with a doctorate in accounting. She had extensive experience in finance. "If you have problems with your account—"

"Can you do an audit?" she asked.

"Yes, ma'am, but I'd suggest hiring—"

"I want to hire you," Miss Genny insisted. "Can you come by in the morning? And keep this just between us."

"I can come by around eight," Ryan replied. "I can't do the job, but we can discuss what the problem is and schedule the actual audit for the weekend."

Miss Genny put her hand on Ryan's arm. "Thanks, Ryan. Meet me at the front entrance."

"Yes, ma'am," she replied wondering what could possibly be going wrong for the other woman to want an audit.

"And stop watching my niece's backside," she said sternly. "She's not on the market."

"Yes, ma'am," Ryan said with a grin. "But she's too pretty not to at least check out."

Miss Genny frowned, shaking her head. "Ryan, no. She can't be seen cavorting around town on a handsome butch's arm being the talk of the town."

"We'd hardly be cavorting," Ryan balked. But she knew the other woman was right about one thing.

Her niece would be the next big topic of conversation. She was a new girl in town, and even now almost two months later men were still falling all over themselves for a date with her. In part, Ryan knew that was because Amelia had been so elusive or rather unavailable.

She was never without Miss Genny except at Willow Inn, the inn owned by Miss Genny. There, Ryan had dined with her several times finding Amelia sitting by herself in a shady corner looking so alone it had made her heart ache.

"Just promise me you'll not make any moves on her," Miss Genny said.

Ryan looked past her to where Amelia stood with her back to them as she chatted with Nan at Nan's booth. Amelia was gorgeous in her simple top and shorts with legs that seemed to go on for miles despite the fact Amelia couldn't be more than five-foot-seven which was just three inches shorter than her.

The sun played through her fine hair making it look like copper set on fire. Amelia turned then, and their eyes met. The connection was a punch to the gut that had Ryan sucking in a breath as tingles rippled down her arms.

Amelia's lips parted slightly, the pink of her gloss making them appear wet.

Wet and kissable.

The things she could do with that body...

"It's not that I don't think you're good enough for her, it's complicated," Miss Genny said in a quiet tone, looking pensive.

"Understood," Ryan answered tearing her gaze from the green one that practically held her ensnared by the desire that flashed in those eyes. "But you can't stop me from looking," She winked at the other woman.

"You're such a guy, Ryan Baptist," she said in mock irritation before striding away, going to join the owner of the small but very successful law firm.

Ryan shook her head. Miss Genny was something else. Some people didn't like her, but most people didn't know her the way Ryan did. She'd never been anything but nice to her. So, Ryan wouldn't make any moves on her niece, at least not this week.

Chapter One

Three Weeks Later.

Amelia Rose-Brier glanced around the old barn that had been renovated and turned into an event hall of some kind. The music was turned up but not blaring and everyone was decked out in an array of clothing styles from the simple jeans and cowboy boots to the dressier dress.

She was right at home in the simple dress she'd bought with its rounded neckline and just above the knee length skirt.

She hadn't made many friends in the nearly four months she'd been here in Avon Del, so she'd had to go shopping alone which was the actual story of her life. At home, she didn't have any real friends, so she spent most of her time alone.

Coming here had been a respite from the fake life she'd been trapped in, and Amelia was falling in love with the simplicity of Avon Del despite not having seen much of it. Then, again, she'd been working hard for her aunt at her inn.

Her Aunt Genny had asked Amelia to come down to help her out in July, and Amelia had come to love working at the inn more each day. But she couldn't stay indefinitely, and she knew it.

"Good evening, ladies," Alston Barrett said. "Can I get you ladies some punch?"

Amelia turned her gaze on the older man with golden skin and sandy hair whose hazel eyes shone with warmth. He wore a button down with tie and slacks looking just as handsome in his relaxed garb as he did in his suit.

"Not just yet," Genny said.

"Well, how about a dance then," he said, and Amelia glanced around wondering if either of the ladies she knew was here.

"Amelia, I think Hope is over there with Kailey," Alston said.

Her gaze swung to his. "Oh, thanks. Aunt Genny, do you mind?"

"No. Go ahead," she said with a smile. "Have some fun. You deserve it. You worked hard this week."

This week she'd put in long hours cleaning rooms and helping with a party. Amelia was enjoying working for her aunt even though her job wasn't sexy. She was here to help and enjoy some time away from the rigorous social life her mother had imposed on her.

Amelia spotted the two women she'd become friendly with. One of them worked at the inn and had introduced her to the other.

As she crossed the room, she caught sight of the very handsome Ryan Baptist clad in worn jeans and a black button down with short sleeves. Her hair, shoulder length dreadlocks were pulled back from her face calling even more attention to copper eyes set in a coffee with cream face.

There was just so much to love about her.

Ryan was in great shape, a great dresser, and Amelia liked the clean citrus scent of her. They'd shared more than a couple of long looks over the summer, and Ryan had seemed to be going out of her way on Mondays and Wednesdays to show up at the inn's restaurant when Amelia was on duty serving.

They'd even shared a table a few times during the crowded lunch hour on Amelia's day off. They had talked, getting friendly enough for Amelia to say hello to her when she saw her. Those sparse moments had sparked attraction in Amelia that she had no idea what to do with.

Ryan's head turned then, and their eyes met. Amelia's heart started to beat fast and her skin heated, her cheeks getting hot. Ryan gave her a nod, and Amelia looked quickly away and hurried over to the two women.

"Hey, Amelia," Hope said with a smile. "Nice dress. Is that one of the ones you picked up at Nan's a few weeks ago?"

She'd bought several things from Nan's on impulse. Amelia knew she'd never wear them, but she had been caught up in a moment.

A moment of foolish stupidity in thinking one of those sexy dresses would inspire Ryan to ask her out.

And she couldn't even go out with her not the way she wanted. Her mother wouldn't find it too distasteful for her to be seen with a woman who was a friend. And that was all she could call any relationship she might want with another woman.

"Yeah."

"It's gorgeous," Kailey said. "She always gets the best stuff in. It's just kind of pricey, but your aunt can afford it, right?"

"I guess." She shrugged.

Kailey reminded her of some of the women her mother insisted she spend time with at home. They were social climbers who only seemed to care about money, social status, and the right last name.

"Glad you came," Hope said. "You look great and there are plenty of guys here who want to dance with you, and probably a handful of women too."

She gave Hope a startled look. "Women?"

"Yeah," Kailey said with a grin, and she caught her hand. "The gay community here isn't that big, but it's alive. In fact, none of us have any problems strutting our stuff on the dance floor at public events."

"True," Hope agreed with a smile. "There's one les club here called Girl Anonymous. It's really cool."

"I'd be there right now if it wasn't for the five-dollar fee which is going to support the food drive."

"How?"

"Well, the money collected will be used to stock the pantry. Pretty much every business in town does some kind of event or participates in one that raises funds for the food bank and the shelter."

"Oh." Amelia nodded.

"The club is discreet," Hope told her. "I don't hang out there much, but Kailey goes a few times a week."

Lesbians?

Amelia didn't have any lesbian friends at home. She was too afraid someone would find out, and she'd lose her job.

The school where she worked was conservative. They'd find a way to fire her without using her sexual orientation. Not only that, but word could also get back to her mother who was threatening her every other day with loss of her inheritance if Amelia so much as looked at a woman too long.

She didn't know if she feared losing her inheritance or her job most.

"And I'm going over tonight too," Kailey said. "Want to come?" She gave Amelia's hand a shake before releasing it.

"Not a good idea for me."

"Your aunt won't mind. She knows we're lesbians," Kailey said. "Come on. One of you has to come with me."

"Not me," Hope said. "So, I guess you're on your own."

"Well, you two stay here then," she said. "And keep pining Hope because that woman is never going to give you the time of day. Not that she's worth it or have you forgotten she's one of the dirty dykes."

Hope sighed. "I know what people call them," Hope muttered. "But they don't know them."

"Who could really?" Kailey demanded. "They walk around here like they're god's gift especially Ryan. It's like she thinks she's too good for us just because she went away to college."

"K—"

"Hell, she couldn't even hack it," Kailey cut in. "Ryan was some kind of Wall Street whiz until it all got to be too much for her, and she came running back home broke with her tail between her legs, and so did her friends."

Amelia's gaze slipped from Kailey to travel across the room to where Ryan was chatting with a group of women.

"Why do they call them dirty dykes?" Amelia asked curiously.

"They like to share their women," Kailey said. "I mean, they're so butch, they wear strap-ons sometimes. Ryan's probably wearing one tonight, but it's not like she's going to use it."

"Maybe they just don't want to go out with you," Hope said coldly.

"Get real, Hope, Ryan is never going to give you the time of day and neither is Charlie, but you can hang around here all night if you want. I'm going to have some real fun. Amelia?"

"Not tonight," she said.

If the club was known as a lesbian hangout, she couldn't go. What if her mother found out? She had threatened to get her fired more than once if she heard she'd been to any lesbian club or out with any woman.

It kept her isolated and right where her mother seemed to want her. Unable to have the life she wanted.

"Too bad," Kailey said. "See you at work tomorrow."

"Have fun." Hope gave her a wave. "She can be a bit jerky sometimes. Ryan Baptist, and Charlie aren't really that bad. They just aren't interested in her."

"That happens," Amelia commented, and Ryan looked her way then and her pulse rushed.

"And it pisses her off that it's happening with them," Hope murmured.

"Why is she so interested in them?" Her skin heated as Ryan's gaze left hers to slowly slide down her as if she was undressing with her mind.

"Rena, one of Ryan's friends owns her own business and makes a pretty penny from what I've heard. Charlie is just hot. She's an insurance adjuster or something. Ryan works at the bank, but she's clearly hot."

"True," Amelia commented breathlessly, nipples peaking from Ryan's gaze, it was like a caress over her bare skin.

"She hasn't seriously dated anyone in almost a year though, and she's brushed Kailey off more than once."

"Oh. For Bobbi-Sue from Old Brier Farms?" She tore her gaze from Ryan's as her clit firmed and her juices gathered wetting her panties. God the woman was going to make her come just from looking at her.

Hope laughed. "Bobbi-Sue hasn't been in the picture for a long time. She cheated on Ryan more than once, and Ryan finally broke up with her."

Bobbi-Sue had been a little catty when she'd run into her at Nan's.

"I'll be right back," Hope murmured.

Once Hope was gone, Amelia threw another glance Ryan's way, and Ryan winked at her. Amelia quickly turned away and made her way over to the bar to get a cup of punch. The cute kid serving gave her a smile.

"Hi, Amelia," he said.

"Hi, Freddie." The kid worked at the inn in the dining room. Now that school had started, he was there only a few hours a day.

"Punch, soda, or wine?" he asked. "Or beer?"

"Punch," she said.

He filled a small cup with a ladle. "Since this is the first time you've been out at a party, lots of guys are scoping you out," he said.

"Oh, really?"

"Really." He grinned. "I wouldn't be surprised if you didn't leave with a phone full of numbers."

"Hey Freddie."

"Hey, Ry," he answered warmly. "I'm surprised you didn't take off yet."

"It's going to be a short night for me, buddy," she told him. "I have to work half a day tomorrow."

"Banker's hours," he said in a teasing tone. "Gives you plenty of time to raise some hell with the rest of them."

She laughed. "Just get me some punch, kid," she ordered lightly.

He handed her a cup. "You met Miss Genny's niece?" he asked.

"Course," she said. "Hi, Amelia."

"Hi." She gave Ryan a smile.

"Thanks, Freddie," Ryan said. "Come on Amelia let's go hold up a wall until someone asks you to dance."

"I'll have a break in ten minutes," Freddie said.

"You're too young to be hitting on her, kid," Ryan said. "Save it for the girls your own age."

"You're such a killjoy."

"Saving you the embarrassment," she said. "You should shalom me."

He laughed. "You just want her for yourself."

"No law against spending a few minutes with a pretty girl. Get back to work," she said and took Amelia's elbow and led her to a corner of the barn where two other women were seated on bales of hay.

"Hi, Amelia," Elise Banks said giving her a smile.

She'd met Elise at the inn.

"Hi."

"This is my wonderful honey, Rena. Rena this is Amelia."

"Who doesn't seem to get out much," Rena commented.

"Ree," Elise said in a chastising tone. "She was only supposed to be here helping out for the summer."

"That wasn't stopping her from taking in the beauty beyond the inn's borders," Ree said and took a drink from the bottle in her hand.

"Ree, chill," Ryan said.

"Addy does all the work," Ree commented.

"I think that's why my aunt asked me to stay," Amelia said. "Addy can't do it all. My aunt said the assistant manager up and left town without any word. She asked me to take the job."

"That's great," Elise said. "How long are you staying."

"Till the end of the year," Amelia answered. "She said she'd hire someone by then."

"There are a few people who will be glad to take that job," Elise said. "Miss Genny pays pretty well I hear."

"I've heard that too," Amelia replied. She was getting paid now that she'd decided to stay. She had declined but her aunt had insisted.

"Saw you hanging with Kailey and Hope," Ree said. "Be careful with Kailey, she's a bit of a gossip."

"Ree," Elise chastised. Kailey's okay. She's just a little upset that my baby and this cutie—" She ran a hand up Ryan's arm. "won't go out with her."

"Hope mentioned that," she said with a frown noticing the way Ryan took Elise's hand. "Uh, so why is the dance being held here?" Amelia tore her gaze away from their joined hands, fighting jealousy.

"It's just the place most of the dances are held," Elise answered. "There was a fire at the Hall last year and it's been rebuilt, but everybody got used to this place. Lot of us pitched in to renovate it for a wedding, and it just kind of became the place to hang out."

"Oh." Amelia struggled to tear her gaze from the joined hands, something inside her wanting to rip Elise apart for making a simple gesture look so intimate.

"It's kind of like that old line shack out near the lake," Ree said. "Kids love to sneak up there and get up to no good."

Amelia smiled. "Make out."

"Right." Elise laughed. "That's why they call it Make Out Woods."

"Are you serious?"

"Sure," Elise responded. "There are various hideaways up there—some even the new generation don't know about, where you can make out or even get naked."

Amelia blushed.

Elise grinned. "We could have a full-scale sex party. You want to ride up there and check out the moon? There's a great view."

"To the woods?" Amelia asked skeptically.

"City girls," Ryan muttered giving her a teasing look and her skin heated.

God. She had to get this under control. It wasn't like she'd never been with a woman before. Just not in months, but she wasn't a virgin.

"Come on," Elise said. "You can ride with us. Ryan can take you home after. Right, Ry?" Elise leaned into Ree as she gave Ryan's hand a light tug.

"Sure," Ryan said. "I won't be long though."

"Come on, Ry," Elise murmured. "We might skinny dip in the creek."

"Go ahead," Ryan replied with a grin. "But I don't think Amelia's taking off a shoe let alone her dress."

"She might," Elise said. "It's still a pretty warm evening, and I bet she's wearing some pretty lingerie she'd love for us to ogle."

Amelia's cheeks heated, and Elise laughed.

"Look at those pink cheeks. I hit the nail right on the head. Come with us."

"I—Hope—"

"She'll be fine," Elise said. "We can invite her next time. Go tell Miss Genny you're going for a ride. We'll take good care of you. I promise." She grinned.

"I—"

"It's just a little outing," Elise cut in.

"Okay," Amelia agreed carefully, her gaze going to Ryan. What harm could there be in a little trip?

"Meet us in the parking lot, Ry," Elise commanded.

"Why not," Ryan said.

They walked across the room, Amelia's heart hammering. She was actually going to be in a park in the dark with Ryan Baptist?

And her friends. One of which seemed like she would climb all over Ryan if she got the chance. Maybe this was a bad idea.

The last thing she wanted was to watch Elise making out with Ryan, and why wasn't Rena upset?

"Hey, Miss Genny. Hi Mr. Alston."

"Ryan, you look quite handsome," Alston said. "Did you pick up a raffle ticket?"

"Yes, sir," she said with a smile.

"Aunt Genny, Elise invited me to hang out with them for a little bit."

"Elise and Rena?" she asked carefully.

"Yes." Amelia nodded catching the worry in her aunt's blue eyes. However, she decided not to ask. She was going to be here until the end of the year. She needed to make a few more friends than Hope and Kailey.

"I can drop Amelia off at her place after," Ryan said. "We won't be long. I have to work in the morning."

"Ryan," her aunt said. "Excuse us for a minute?" Her aunt motioned to Ryan.

Amelia frowned. Now, she was really concerned. Was her aunt going to warn Ryan off and why?

Chapter Two

"Ryan, this isn't a good idea," Miss Genny said coldly. "Amelia's not like some of the other girls you three have played around with. She has no idea that—"

"Miss Genny, Elise invited her, but nothing's going to happen."

"Right. Elise is known for luring other girls into your menage or orgy web."

Ryan laughed. "She's a grown woman, Miss Genny and if she says no, nothing will happen, I can promise you that."

"It better not, and you three better not talk this all over town," she said angrily. "She's not—She couldn't deal with that."

"We never talk," Ryan told her, allowing a chill into her voice. They were always discreet. It was the townspeople who imagined they knew what went on between the three of them, well, four and other women.

Ree and Elise enjoyed a menage, but it never meant anything. Yeah, women misread Elise and got hurt, but she wouldn't allow Amelia to be one of them.

"Promise me, you'll take care of her," Miss Genny demanded.

"Promise," Ryan agreed. And she would.

"Don't forget to stop by for that talk," Miss Genny said. "I'm eager to know what you've found."

Ryan nodded grimly. She had done the audit last week and gone over her findings last night. She'd been too busy to work on the side project with her boss thrusting another colleague's work off on her. The job had involved a trip out of town for a week.

"I'll give you the run down then," Ryan said. "And nothing will happen Amelia—"

"I want her to ride with you," she interjected. "Do whatever you need to, say whatever makes sense to avoid her being alone with them. Elise's reputation is even worse than the three of yours."

Ryan nodded somberly. Elise was bi-sexual and already had quite a reputation even before they'd become friends with her.

"Will do. I'll come over around one. I can grab some lunch," Ryan said. "I hope you've ordered some pies from Bailey's because your cook can't make a potato pie for s—for a song."

Genny waggled a finger at her. "Ryan Baptist," she said in a chastising tone. "You just take care of my niece. She's sweet, and she deserves someone to care about her not get her head all messed up over nonsense."

"I'd never mess her head up over nonsense," Ryan said with a grin.

Genny waggled a finger at her. "Not just you, but Elise."

"I'll take care of her," Ryan promised. She wouldn't allow Amelia to wade into the deep waters of one-nightstands and flings with Elise and Ree. Not tonight. If that's what Amelia was after, she'd have to do that on her own.

Miss Genny gave her a satisfied nod and led the way back to where Amelia was watching them, looking more than a little mortified. Alston gave her a smile.

"Don't be too late, Amelia," Genny said.

"I won't," she murmured.

With a wave they were heading from the barn to the parking lot. Music was playing and a group of kids were hanging out laughing and talking. Amelia thought she picked up the distinct smell of weed.

Ryan took her elbow and steered her further away and Amelia was glad. She hated the smell of that stuff.

"Kids being kids," Ryan said.

"You got high when you were their age?"

"I did some pot," she said. "But most kids have tried it at least once."

"Not me," Amelia admitted. She'd never been drunk either. Never been in trouble with the cops. Never even broke curfew at home or at boarding school.

"Hey, guys," Elise said. "I was about to message you to see what was taking so long."

"Miss Genny," Ryan said.

"Ride with us Amelia," Elise said with a smile.

"We'll meet you there," Ryan said. "Miss Genny's orders."

Elise laughed.

"Come on, sweetie." Ree opened the door for her, and Elise climbed in.

Ryan led her to her truck. This was going to be an interesting hour or so.

****

"This is me," Ryan said stopping at a pick-up truck. She unlocked the door and pulled it open for Amelia.

"Thanks." She climbed in and Ryan was in on the other side within seconds.

She started the truck and backed out. "Nothing wrong with that," Ryan said at last. "Good girls don't put a toe out of line."

"That's kind of insulting," Amelia commented, brows knitting on her forehead.

"Yeah? Why? You got caught smoking cigarettes?"

"No." She made a face.

"Drunk or sneaking out?"

"No."

"Stretched out on the bed with a girl between your legs learning some night moves?"

"Night what?" Amelia asked with a frown.

"Experimenting."

"My mom caught me kissing a girl once." And that had been the beginning of the emotional reins her mother kept on her.

Ryan laughed. "What happened?"

"I got sent to a gender affirming camp for six weeks."

"That was extreme," Ryan said.

"It wasn't a nice place," she murmured. "They called it a Christian camp, but they expected me to have sex with a couple of men. I refused despite their threats to tell my mom I was fooling around with one of the girls there."

"Were you?"

"We were all too afraid to do anything," she said softly. "I never gave my mother any reason to doubt I'd changed, but because I wouldn't date, she stayed on my case. Fixed me up with boys and then men."

"You haven't come out to her?"

"She knows I'm not straight, but she refuses to accept it, and she refuses to allow me to be who I am."

"How's she doing that?' Ryan asked, confusion in her tone.

"I could lose my job at the school where I work if they find out I'm a lesbian. It's a conservative school. The headmaster thinks if any kid expresses or appears to be gay that it's his duty to jerk them back in line and make sure they understand they're going to hell."

"That is shit," Ryan muttered. "I despise people like that. There are more than enough around here in the two churches, but they can kiss my ass."

Amelia laughed.

Ryan grunted. "Your mother has issues, baby."

"She has issues with me that's for sure," Amelia murmured.

"You're here until the end of the year, right?" Ryan asked as she pulled into a parking lot and cut the engine.

"Yes."

Ryan released her seatbelt and shifted in her seat to face Amelia. Amelia studied her, thinking Ryan's brown eyes reflected light as if they were backlit. She pushed the thought away as a sign of having read way too many romances about werewolves.

"You're too pretty to waste your time on a man, baby," she said softly. "I'm not going to tell you to throw your life away. Only you know your circumstances. But if I were you, I'd have some fun before I went back home. Enough to last me through the cold days ahead."

"Kailey offered to take me to a club, but if my mom finds out..."

"You don't have to be public," Ryan said. "There's nothing wrong with having a secret lover as long as she's down with it." Ryan climbed out of the truck and came around to her side and opened her door.

Amelia got out and leaned against the door after Ryan closed it. She looked up at her but noticed the silence all around. Well, the absence of humans.

She looked up at the sky and could almost see the moon through the heavy branches of towering trees.

"Let's go," Ryan said. "The view's this way."

Amelia followed Ryan into the trees. Ryan put a hand on her back making her shiver.

"Careful, there are a few down limbs."

"Thanks."

As they made their way through the trees, Amelia picked up faint sounds of laughter. She was suddenly in no hurry to see the moon or Elise and Rena.

They walked for several minutes before Ryan stopped and pointed.

"There," Ryan said.

Amelia looked up, gaze filling with the sight of the moon and the silver flecks dotting the midnight-colored canvas.

"Beautiful," she breathed as she leaned against the trunk of a tree.

"The cover of night can be a lonely woman's best friend," Ryan murmured, and Amelia looked at her.

"Are you applying for the job?" she asked quietly not bothering to deny she was lonely.

What would be the point?

Ryan might not know she was so lonely she cried herself to sleep at night from the desperation, the anger with herself, and the unhappiness. However, Amelia knew it was all over her face sometimes even when all she wanted to do was hide.

Ryan lifted her brows, a question clear in her brown eyes.

"The job of being my secret lover."

Chapter Three

Ryan leaned close to her putting a hand on the trunk of the tree giving Amelia a good whiff of the clean scent of her.

"I can be discreet, but do you really want to play with me?"

"You think you're out of my league?" Amelia challenged.

"I might be."

"Maybe I'm out of yours," she said. "Maybe you don't think you can handle me."

Ryan laughed, her eyes alight with humor, but there was a subtle challenge in her depths that made Amelia want to accept that dare even though she knew Ryan was right.

Ryan was out of her league. She didn't have half the experience with women or relationships she might have had had she been brave enough to defy her mother.

"You might be in some ways," Ryan murmured leaning a little closer. "But if you want to play, I'm game. I just want to know one thing. What are you trying to prove?"

"I don't have to prove anything except that I can live on my terms," Amelia told her. "After talking to my mother today, I realized I was tired." Tired. Angry. "Mostly, I'm afraid of never experiencing real love." The kind she read about in books and heard in songs. "I want a life that makes me happy."

"And a fling with me could be that first start."

"Ry—"

"I don't mind helping you find yourself," Ryan cut in, no recrimination in her tone. "But just make sure you know what you're doing and why."

"You're the one who said I should have some fun before I left, so maybe I want to do all the things I probably will never get to do."

"I'm game," Ryan said with a shrug. "I don't mind helping a damsel in distress."

"This damsel wants to be kissed. She wants a girlfriend even if it's-it's—"

"Not as organic as it could be," Ryan said when she broke off.

Amelia nodded, lowering her gaze expecting Ryan to laugh at her.

"Hey," Ryan said, gripping her chin and lifting it. "Amelia, look at me."

Ryan's fingers were soft on her skin, and Amelia met Ryan's gaze, fear a tight knot in her stomach.

"Yes?" Her voice was quiet, uncertainty playing through her.

Ryan's thumb moved gently on her chin, caressing. "Being lonely and wanting someone who wants to focus on you isn't a crime."

"Can you do—I mean—" She broke off again, her cheeks on fire now.

Ryan gave her a wicked grin. "Yeah." She nodded and lowered her head.

"Don't just humor me."

"I have no intentions of that," Ryan told her, her lips against Amelia's.

"I mean it," Amelia said breathlessly. "I want to be enjoyed, to enjoy."

She wanted to release the passion smashed down into a box inside her. The passion that made her want to catch fire and burn uncontrolled.

Their lips met in a soft kiss that had Amelia's stomach quivering. Her hand moved to rest on Ryan's hip. It had been so long since she'd actually kissed a woman let alone had sex that her entire body seemed to come alive in a big yawning sigh.

Her skin warmed, her heart beat faster. Amelia parted her lips, and Ryan's tongue swept inside, gliding along her own in a sensual slide that made her wet and her nipples harden.

Amelia strained closer and the pent-up need inside her became a flame that burned through her common sense. Her other hand glided up Ryan's back to her nape. Her fingers stroked before pushing into the dreadlocks.

The kiss became heated, turning Amelia's skin into a living flame as her juices dampened her panties and the hard points of her nipples pressed painfully against the cups of her bra.

Ryan's lips moved from hers to the corner of her mouth to her jaw. Her tongue licked along Amelia's throat, and Amelia caught her breath, the hunger intensifying in her.

Ryan claimed her mouth again, the kiss demanding, but Ryan's hands rested on the tree rather than on her making Amelia want to scream.

Touch me, she begged silently. I need your touch.

Then, Ryan's hands were on her hips, sliding down to her thighs. Ryan plundered her mouth, the kiss drugging even as Ryan pushed the skirt of her dress up and pushed her hand inside Amelia's panties.

Ryan's fingers whispered over the plump lips of her pussy drawing a moan from Amelia as she shivered. Ryan slipped a finger past her labia, the tip tracing a path from her clit down to the opening of her body to slip into the slick humid depths.

Amelia creamed, her body already preparing itself for the delicious penetration to come as Ryan's lips moved on her neck, kissing her. She sucked, the sensation an erotic pull that made her blood quicken. Ryan could hear it rushing in her ears, feel something inside her scratching at her mind to be free even as Ryan pressed her finger deeper into Amelia's pussy.

Amelia moaned, the rapture of the caress making her wetter. "Ryan." Ryan's name came out a needy plea.

Amelia knew she should stop this. They hardly even knew each other, and this wasn't a proper first date. However, having sex here was an illicit and forbidden act and the very thought of public sex made her wetter.

She wanted to do everything...everything she had ever wanted but wouldn't out of fear.

Ryan drew her finger out and pressed her thumb against Amelia's clit, drew it around and barely grazed it before sliding two fingers into the tight sheath sending pleasure ricocheting through her.

The caress created a wave of heat over her skin that caused sweat to dew her forehead.

I want you.

"I want you too, baby," Ryan murmured in her ear and nipped Amelia's ear lobe and drew her fingers out only to glide them back in while her thumb worked her clit in wicked circles.

A needy sound escaped Amelia, her eyes closing, her body arching into the caress, the need a powerful ache. Ryan thrust her fingers in again and ground the heel of her hand against the tight knot of Amelia's pleasure button as she found a steady rhythm.

"Oh god," Amelia breathed as she put her hand on Ryan's. "Ryan."

"Look at me, Amelia," Ryan ordered. "Share your passion with me."

Her lashes fluttered up and her gaze met the dark chocolate of Ryan's. The dark pools held her ensnared and her entire world was centered right here, right now in this moment where time stood still, and pleasure was a beautiful melody.

"That's what I want," Ryan murmured. "to see those pretty eyes all dark with heat." Ryan's fingers drove into her, and Amelia moaned, her nails digging into the back of Ryan's wrist.

Ryan's fingers were deft in their movements taking control of her body leaving Amelia mindless.

"Your cat is so tight around my fingers, begging to be taken, baby," Ryan murmured thickly.

Amelia could only feel, catch fire.

Ryan's touch was masterful, her clit a pulsing knot, and she put her hand on Ryan's, her nails biting into Ryan's skin. Amelia couldn't stop the rake over the back of Ryan's hand or the urge to mark her that seized her in a tight grip.

"Damn the smell of your pussy is so sweet," Ryan crooned.

"Ryan," she cried. Her fingers were so good inside her, Amelia didn't want it to end.

Mewling, Amelia's head rolled from side to side on the tree's thick trunk and then her body pulled tight, the pressure on her clitoris unbearable and her nails locked in Ryan's wrist as she came with a low gasp.

The tide of pleasure swept her away, drowning out all sound. The scent of blood was faint and something inside her lifted its head as the fires of desire continued to consume her.

Then, Amelia's knees weakened, and she slumped against the tree. Ryan curved an arm around her, pulling her against her, and held her as she drew her fingers from her tight clench.

Breathing hard, Amelia rested her head against Ryan's shoulder taking pleasure in the warmth and strength of her. The scent of her was incredible now, it made her want to wrap herself around her like a blanket.

That had been the best orgasm she'd ever had, and it wouldn't be the last with Ryan if she had anything to say about it.

Chapter Four

The next morning, Ryan walked into her kitchen with a smile, Amelia flitting through her mind. She was a beautiful woman, and Ryan suspected there was more to her than the shy woman she saw.

She put her phone on the table and then started coffee and sat down at the table with her paper while she waited for it to perk. She read the first page, and the chatter about the success of the event last night. As she moved on to another story, her phone rang snagging her attention.

She picked it up. A glance at the display, and Ryan just stared at the unrecognizable number.

"Hello?"

"Hello, Ryan," a calm voice murmured in her ear.

"Hello, Uncle Mihai," she said evenly. The older man was her father's best friend. She'd met him before her mother's death.

Her father had been part of her life before he was killed. After his death, his best friend, Uncle Mihai, had spent time with her on and off.

"How are you?" he asked, the Romanian accent no longer noticeable.

"I'm fine, and how are you?" she asked. "You sound a bit subdued."

"It's hot here in this part of the country for fall."

She smiled. "I suppose it is. Do you need something?" Mihai was a vampire who rarely came out in the light despite having an amulet that allowed him to walk among humans without suffering burns.

She got up to pour herself a cup of coffee as she waited for his response. Ryan added cream and a pinch of sugar before going back to the table.

"I need to see you," he said. "I've heard you were seeing a Thistle-Rose."

"No. She's just Miss Genny's niece." She stirred the hot brew.

"She's not just Genevieve's niece," Mihai replied softly. "She's a Rose-Brier."

"Uncle Mihai, what are you talking about? Amelia isn't like us."

"Us?" His voice held a hint of derision. "You're one of them, and I'm one of us."

She rolled her eyes. "My father—"

"Your mother is the reason you're one of them."

"Did you call just to try to make me feel inferior?" she asked coldly. "or do you have an actual reason."

"Come see. I'm at the coven stead."

"I—" Her other line rang. "Uncle Mihai—"

"Come to me later," he told her. I must sleep now. The sun is draining me."

She sighed and ended the call. "Hello?" she asked absently. Ryan couldn't imagine what Mihai wanted to see her about.

She was even more confused as to why he called her about Amelia. She was human not a vampire like them. She would have noticed that last night, but Amelia had been all soft and needy woman against that tree.

Damn, but she'd smelled so enticing Ryan had thrown her resolution against casual sex to the wind.

"What's going on?"

Ryan swallowed the sip of coffee as she sat at the table positioned next to a wall in her medium sized kitchen.

"Just having coffee, what's up with you?"

"Chilling," Rena said in her ear. "What are you doing today?"

"Uh, why?"

"I was wondering if you'd like to come over for dinner today and bring Amelia of course. Charlie's coming. She's supposed to be bringing a date."

"I—"

"I'm just throwing some steaks on the grill, uh, Charlie's bringing the drinks. You can get dessert."

"I'll ask if she wants to come," Ryan said.

"I'm sure she wants to come," Rena said in a teasing tone. "Looks like you had her coming pretty hard last night."

"Rena."

That hadn't been the plan, but then they'd had that conversation. And the scent of her had been incredible. Not the perfume, that had been nice too, but the natural smell of Amelia's skin. It had been like-like pheromones.

An inescapable lure she couldn't resist.

Rena's laughter cut into her thoughts. "When did you start fooling around with her?"

"None of your business," Ryan replied lazily. Since she'd started looking for someone special, she'd given up casual sex, but last night she hadn't been able to help herself.

She'd told herself that slip had happened because it had been more than six months since she'd enjoyed a woman. It wasn't that she had high standards. It was more the fact she didn't want sex to muddy the waters of a relationship.

"Doesn't matter, Miss Genny is going to break that shit up. I don't think she thinks anyone around here is good enough for the princess."

"What?" Ryan asked incredulously.

"Yeah, it's like she's been deliberately keeping anyone who might be interested at bay."

"Maybe it's not Miss Genny." Genny had warned her off a couple of times, but what ultimately did or didn't happen between her, and Amelia was Amelia's decision.

Rena snorted. "Don't flatter yourself. I'm sure Rapunzel's let her hair down a few times but if you think you're anything special, think again."

"Stop being such an ass," she responded coolly. "Amelia's okay. She's just a little shy."

More like afraid to live, but if she wanted to come down from the tower or invite her in, Ryan was more than happy to spend time with her. She wasn't under any illusions about where this might go.

She was certain Amelia would be heading home at the end of the year to do exactly as her mother wanted. She wasn't the first woman Ryan had met who wanted to have one last fling before she settled down with a man to raise a couple of kids.

Even today, it took courage to be who you were in a world where different really wasn't appreciated. They were just lucky that here in Avon Del being gay, while frowned on, didn't get them hurt. It might get them ridiculed by some, but it didn't put them in real danger.

"Well, if you like her, it's cool," Rena said. "Elise likes her, and no she's not interested in sleeping with her. We're putting that on the back burner."

"Really? Why?"

"We both want to settle down, have kids," she replied quietly, and Ryan could hear the longing in her friend's voice. "I mean, we still plan to swing once in a while, but we want to spend more time getting to know each other. The menages and stuff are getting in the way."

"It's about time," Ryan said with a smile. She had nothing against a menage. They were fun, but polyamorous relationships weren't for her.

"I know. Maybe we're just growing up or some shit."

Ryan chuckled. "Maybe."

Elise and Rena had been dating since she and Rena had moved back here five years ago. They'd gone to college in Atlanta and had both gotten jobs right out of college in New York. Charlie had come home after college, but the three of them had stayed in touch.

"So, come by around three. Elise is looking forward to getting to know Amelia. She said she thought you two looked cute together."

Ryan snorted this time. "I'll let you know if we're coming."

"Try to," Rena said. "You know how much I like touching base with you and Charlie once a week."

"Yeah. Okay. Later." She ended the call with a jab of her finger and smiled.

Elise had been good for them both when they'd returned from New York, and Ryan still thought of her as a friend. However, she wasn't sure Elise was the exact right person to settle down with. Ryan didn't think she had it in her, but she'd never tell Ree that.

Ree hadn't had the same kind of loving family as she and Charlie. Ree's parents had engaged in polyamorous relationships and had three other children. Ree had been raised with them all, but not in the most conventional way.

The three of them had been brought together by their witch mothers. Their mothers had been part of the same coven and had all ventured into the subculture of vampirism. As a result, each of them had come into contact with night walking vampires.

They, as children, had been introduced to the vampire coven and gotten to know the subculture in the area. They lived on the fringes of that culture now, none of them having had a desire to live within the bounds of it full on.

Ryan sighed. She could be wading into trouble with Amelia. But today she wanted to see her, so she would. Ryan was certain Miss Genny would warn her off again. However, it was up to Amelia if she stayed gone.

****

Amelia set her teacup down and glanced at her tablet. She was going out to take a few pictures today. She had a few ideas about how to help her aunt increase business, but she needed to see more of the land before she finalized her proposal.

She had come to love working at the inn and was thinking about asking her aunt for a more permanent job.

"Good morning, Amelia."

"Morning," she said looking up when her aunt came into the breakfast room.

"I guess you had fun last evening," she commented, sitting down at the table and pouring herself a cup of tea from the pot on the trivet on the table.

"Did I wake you?" she asked. The house had felt empty when she'd come home last night at ten. Amelia had been more attuned to her environment than she ever had been.

Not just the sounds, but the energy or lack thereof. She'd always been able to sense some things, but last night she had just known she was alone.

"No." Her aunt gave her a smile as she added a splash of milk to her tea. "I'm just surprised you went with them. I know your mother has plans for you."

Amelia took a sip of her tea. "I don't think I'm interested in her plans even though it might cost me my inheritance."

"Oh? What are you thinking of doing?"

"I like it here. I know it's only been a few months, but Avon Del feels like home."

Her aunt smiled. "You're welcome to stay. I love having you here. In fact, I could use you through next year. I'm thinking of taking an extended trip to Europe. You'd be in charge."

"Are you—That would be fantastic," Amelia burst out. "I would love that."

"But there's a catch."

"What is it?" Amelia asked warily. There was always a catch and it always involved sacrifice on her part.

"You'd have to stay on the full year," she said. "I mean, that would give me time to train your replacement when you decided to leave."

"That wouldn't be a problem," Amelia answered. Moving here was her chance to find her own place in the world and escape the bonds weighing her spirit and slowly destroying her emotionally.

"As to Ryan, I won't interfere if you're going to be seeing her, but I would advise you to use discretion."

"I know Mom would have a fit, but—"

"Sweetheart, you're at liberty to live your life as you see fit because when it all comes down to it, it's ourselves we have to be at peace with not the world around us."

She nodded. "Thanks, Aunt Genny. Mom thinks I should marry Greg Lorkin."

"The Lorkins are an okay family," she said. "A bit on the snobby side, but they're right where your mother's family wants you to be."

"In every way," Amelia responded quietly. "Greg is a doctor. He graduated from Princeton in the top fifteen percent of his class, he's going into private practice with a couple of other doctors in plastic surgery."

"Can he give you the life you want?"

Amelia frowned, slowly shaking her head. Marrying him, living the life her mother had planned for her would destroy what was left of her will, shattering her spirit.

"Grandfather always seemed so nice, but I have to wonder if he'd be like Mom."

"My father wouldn't shun you because you're gay, Amelia. He'd love you for who you are just as I do. I know the will has handicapped you, and if the money means as much to you as it does to your siblings and your mother and grandmother, then, you're going to have to make some decisions fast."

"I know."

"You need to be prepared to accept them and live with them."

She nodded as she caressed her teacup. "I want to wake happy, Aunt Genny. I don't want to wake up on the verge of tears and go through my day just waiting for it to be over."

If not for her job in the school's library, she would anyway. The job gave her something apart from the life she despised, but it had become just another handcuff tying her to a world she didn't want to be apart of.

"Why would you?" she asked curiously. "Marrying Greg Lorkin could only afford you with privilege."

"Money, wealth buys a whole lot of nice things, but the things won't make me happy. They'll keep me busy. I'll be a popular society wife, but I won't have any friends."

"You have friends."

"Not real ones," she murmured. And certainly, no lover whose very name in her thoughts set her on fire like Ryan's did.

She wanted more of her. She wanted to be tied to her, owned by her, enjoyed by her.

Amelia wanted to spend every moment with Ryan that she wasn't working. And last night had been like a door unlocking and swinging open revealing a room full of potential.

The ring of the bell had her tensing.

"I see," her aunt murmured. "And friendships are important more so than the charities you'll work on? More so than the lives you'll be able to touch?"

Before she could answer, the butler came in. "Miss Honeywell."

"Yes, Bentley?"

"Ryan Baptist is here for Miss Amelia."

Amelia smiled. "Tell Ryan I'll be right there," Amelia said. "Excuse me, Auntie." She was out of her chair and hurrying out of the room. Her heart was thumping loudly in her chest as her blood rushed in excitement.

When Amelia stepped into the foyer, she smiled at the sight of Ryan standing there glancing around. She was clad in casual khaki pants and a short sleeved button-down. Her hair—her hair was soft though she wouldn't have expected that of dreadlocks.

Her mother had always made fun of people with dreadlocks saying they were nasty and hard.

Ryan's hair was soft and almost looked like spiral curls. She had the shoulder length locks pulled back today with a band.

"Hi," Ryan said moving to her. "Don't you look pretty."

Amelia smiled shyly. She wore a simple dress having gone to morning mass with her aunt. She hadn't changed out of anything but her shoes.

"Hi, Ryan," Amelia said. "We went to mass this morning."

"Ah, mass," she said. "So, what's going on the rest of the day?" Ryan slipped one hand into her pants pocket making her look not only relaxed but sexy.

"Uh—" The sound came out breathless. "Lunch with one of my aunt's friends."

"You want to cancel to hang with me and have an early dinner with me and my buddies?"

"Dinner?"

"At Ree's," Ryan said taking her hand.

"I—" She broke off remembering last night. Elise made her a little nervous with her too handsy behavior.

"Hey, you're safe with me," Ryan told her. "Nothing ever has to happen you aren't ready for, okay?"

Amelia nodded.

"Baby, when I ask you a question, I expect a voiced reply," Ryan told her quietly, her brown gaze compelling.

"Okay," Amelia said nodding.

"Do you understand that nothing has to happen you don't want?"

"I understand," she said softly as she averted her gaze. There was something so dominant about Ryan that both compelled and overwhelmed her at once.

"Look at me," Ryan commanded giving her hand a shake.

Amelia met her gaze.

"Are you okay with last night?"

"I'd never say you raped me," she replied. "I know—I'm okay with it."

"You know what?" Ryan queried. "You can say whatever's on your mind with me. I'm a big girl. If I don't like it, I can deal."

"I was just going to say that I know it was probably nothing to you, but it was fantastic."

Ryan laced her fingers through Amelia's. "You were amazing, Amelia, and I can't wait to spend more time with you in bed and out."

The words surprised her, and Amelia looked away. The intensity in Ryan's gaze too much.

"So, how about dinner, and before that?"

Amelia met her gaze. "I'd like to spend the rest of the day with you," she said.

"Great. Is Miss Genny here?"

"Yeah. Why?" Amelia asked carefully.

"I'd like to ask her something."

"She's in the breakfast room." She turned and led Ryan to the breakfast room which was right off the kitchen.

Her aunt was still there with her tea only she had her phone before her and was texting.

"Aunt Genny?"

"Is everything okay with Ryan?" she asked. "You have to be careful being seen with her. There isn't anyone here your mother knows, but she might have hired someone. I'm trying to talk her into letting you stay for the rest of the year and next year."

"Oh. She probably won't agree, but I've already made up my mind," Amelia said, moving further into the room, Ryan still holding her hand.

"Morning, Miss Genny."

"Ryan," she said giving them a startled look.

"I like that dress on you," Ryan said.

Genny narrowed her eyes on her. "You're such a guy, Ryan Baptist," she said wagging a finger at her. "What are you up to? Only a well-trained man no matter his age gives a compliment when he's trying to win a woman over."

Ryan laughed. "What can I say. Daddy raised me right," she said.

"Yes, he did," she agreed. "Your father is a good man. So, what are you up to?"

"I was wondering if you minded us taking out one of your paddle boats and cruising the canal."

"We?"

"Charlie said she'd meet me at the dock if you gave permission. If not, we'll have to head back to my place and go out on the lake."

"That won't be necessary," Genny said somberly. "You three can take a boat out. Amelia's never been out on the canal. Amelia, go change. The paddle boat isn't conducive to that dress."

"Yes, ma'am," she said. "I won't be long, Ryan."

"Take your time," Ryan replied.

Amelia exited the room after a quick look at her aunt. She hoped Ryan would still be there when she got back. However, she had a feeling her aunt was about to send Ryan packing.

****

Have a seat, Ryan," Miss Genny said, and Ryan took the chair opposite the older woman.

She had a feeling this was where Genny read her the riot act.

"I'd like you to come work for me," she said. "I need someone reliable who won't rob me blind."

"What about Leah?" Leah was her current accountant and business manager.

"After going over the results of the audit, I've decided to fire her and considering how much money she's cost me, I'm going to prosecute."

"That's too bad for her."

"If the theft wasn't as sophisticated as it was, and she hadn't—The amount of money is too great for me to ignore."

"No, I understand, I didn't mean you shouldn't prosecute her," Ryan said. "She stole greater than a hundred and fifty thousand dollars, and she was in the process of trying to sell part of your property. I found the communications as well as the forged documents that—"

"You didn't mention that before."

"I didn't have the proof until last night. It came in after I dropped Amelia off."

She nodded, her face hardening. "I'll have her investigated to find out if she was in this alone or if someone else who works for me helped her."

"I'll forward the results to you," Ryan told her. "In the meantime, you should contact the bank and have them deny all her access to your accounts."

"Can you do that for me?"

"I already put it in motion. That's when I found out she had a quarter of a mill transfer from your business account started but it's pending your okay. I had that stopped."

"Thank you. I'll call Alvin Rosewood and have her arrested this morning."

"Why not wait until tomorrow? It's Sunday." She wouldn't be able to get the police chief anyway. He was likely out on the water fishing.

She shook her head, her gaze filled with humor. "I need you to come work for me," she said. "Amelia will need someone to help her while I'm on my trip."

"Trip?"

"To Europe," she replied with a smile. "So, could you take a leave or just quit? I'll pay you more."

"I've been looking for a change, but I was going to take a job with Ree. I handed in my resignation yesterday."

"Tell Ree I need you."

"I'll work it out with her, but the best I'll be able to give you for the next few weeks is an hour or two, three times a week."

"I'll take it," Miss Genny answered with a smile. "Can you come in tomorrow and begin cleaning up that mess?"

"Sure," Ryan agreed. "I'm already familiar with your books after the audit, so it won't take long to put things in order. A week at the snail's pace."

"You have no idea how much I'll appreciate this."

Ryan gave her a grim smile. "I'm happy to help and the inn will be a nice change of pace as well as provide nice scenery."

"Don't give Amelia false hope. I know she's not the kind of woman you're interested in."

"We're just getting to know each other, Miss Genny. Whatever does or doesn't happen is up to Amelia."

"And you," she said. "Don't be too persuasive. She's not the kind of girl who's going to walk away from her name or her life."

"I'd think living her life would be something her family would want."

"As long as she goes home and marries a young man, it is. Otherwise, she'll be disinherited, and her mother won't have much if anything to do with her."

"That'd be unfortunate," Ryan said. "But Amelia's who I'm taking my cues from Miss Genny. Maybe all she needs is time to make sure that life is what she can live with."

"She's going back at the end of next year."

"I'll miss her."

Chapter Five

The breakfast nook was quiet when Amelia returned, and her heart sank.

Ryan was just like all the others. She'd listened to someone else instead of her. Amelia slipped inside prepared to hear whatever explanation her aunt would make for Ryan only to find Ryan seated at the table, eyes on her phone. Her lips curved into a smile, and she looked up as if sensing her there.

Ryan rose, her gaze sliding over her slowly, making Amelia shiver.

"I guess you have something else to do? Work?"

"On a Sunday? Sweetheart I work at a bank. We don't work on Sundays, but now that you mention it—"

"Something you forgot that you had to do?"

Ryan frowned as she moved toward her. "I'm not that forgetful," she said. "Are you ready?"

"Your friend Charlie is joining us, and you know a nice, secluded spot you two want to show me?"

"You have no idea where you are, do you? Your aunt doesn't make half use of this property. She's butted up against a park. It spans three towns, and the views are beautiful. The canal goes right through the park."

"I didn't know."

"The park is something to see, but when the leaves start to change in earnest later this month, and November, you're going to love taking a cruise along the canal."

"Oh."

"Come on," she said. "That was Charlie. She invited Hope."

"Hope?"

Ryan laughed and pulled Amelia into her arms. "What did you think I had in mind? An outdoor orgy with you the star?"

"I'm not sure."

"I admit I've been a bastard, but it's not what I'm about," she said. "If you're going to continuously doubt that, this is going to go from promising to annoying to difficult in about three days."

Amelia studied her. "It's not—I'm used to people wanting to be with me to get close to my family. A job, a recommendation, just something to advance their own position."

Ryan sighed. "Why don't we go ahead and get started if you still want to go," Ryan said.

"I do." Amelia smiled, hope taking wing inside her.

Ryan gave her a nod, and Amelia led her to the foyer and out the front door.

"We'll drive down to the dock," Ryan said. "We won't do much exploring today. You aren't wearing the shoes for it, and neither am I."

"That's fine," Amelia said, thinking that somehow she'd either offended Ryan, or Ryan was regrouping and trying to come up with a lie that would lull her into a false sense of security.

She had really wanted this to be different, but she supposed the best she was going to get out of this was a little fun. Then, she'd turn her attention to the life she wanted to make here. Maybe she'd find someone, maybe not.

That didn't really matter. As lonely as she was, she had gotten very good at being alone.

"I guess Kailey's been telling you all kinds of things about us," Ryan said after they were in her truck and backing out.

"She mentioned a few things."

"She loves to talk, but I think her problem is she wants in to one of our beds. Hell, maybe all three."

"All three?"

"Ree and Elise have never given her the sexual time of day, and Charlie was interested for all of five minutes."

"What about you?"

"Not really. She's attractive, but she's not my type."

"What is your type?" Amelia asked curious.

Ryan put the truck in gear and headed down the driveway. The house was big and was the only one on the street. Amelia had no idea how much land the house sat on, and she hadn't asked. But the nearest neighbor was a good fifteen minutes or so by car at least.

"Today, red heads that think they're too hot for me to handle."

Amelia laughed. "I didn't say that."

"You implied it though," Ryan said.

"Kailey said you used to work on Wall Street?" she asked though she'd meant to merely state.

"Yep," Ryan nodded. "Lots of people think I came home because I couldn't cut it, and they were right in a manner of speaking. Living in New York never did settle good with me. I enjoyed the work, excelled at it, but the rat race got old."

"How do you mean?"

"A few too many times I was forced to do things I didn't agree with just to keep my job," Ryan said. "I woke up one morning and didn't like the materialistic bitch looking back at me in the mirror. I decided I used to be better than that. Still was, somewhere deep inside."

"And you quit your job?"

"Not that day. It was another nine months. I was tossing back gin with my bosses. They were congratulating themselves on being able to deceive the SEC over trading violations. We'd all made a chunk of change over the violations. They were planning to do it again, and they were offering me a big fat raise and partnership."

"You walked away?"

"Two weeks after I made partner. I was the youngest in the firm's history. The hardest working, hungriest kid on the block, I wanted it all." She shook her head. "I wanted to prove I was the best, and I got caught up in the shit. My parents would have been ashamed of me. Hell, I know I was."

"What about your friend who was there?"

"Ree. She has her own reasons for coming home. It's her story to tell, but I can tell you she wasn't out there bad like I was. I was shit."

"I'm sure that's not true," she said trying to decide what Ryan was trying to get her to think or say.

"At the end of the day, I needed to be comfortable with who I was, and I wasn't. Don't get me wrong. I'm still damn proud of my accomplishments in the early part of my career, but I'll never be that woman again."

"Your parents—"

"Have no idea what kind of woman I was in New York, and they'll never find out from me," Ryan said and smiled a ghost of a smile. "Any way, Mom's been gone for years. I was a kid when she passed. My dad raised me."

"Are you two close?"

"Yes," she said with a smile. "Dad remarried and has two girls and a boy. His wife had a hard time dealing with me. She didn't want another woman's kid and especially not one like me."

"Like you?"

"I was a tomboy to the max. I could kick any boy in my grade's ass and did. I could fish, shoot, and loved it. I was a jock too. Baseball, soccer, and even swimming."

Amelia laughed not expecting to hear that. "Are you kidding?"

"Naw. They went a few rounds over me before she pulled herself together and accepted that I was part of his life. Therefore, part of hers if she was going to stick around."

"Sounds like you have a good Dad."

"The old man's cool," she said. "Amelia, I don't need your family's help with my career. I haven't been happy at the bank for a while. It reminds me too much of what I left, but I don't need Miss Genny to do anything for me."

"I—"

"Ree has her own business, and she offered me a job. She makes a good living, and she's willing to make me her partner. The thing is, Miss Genny offered me a job because she's going to need a new accountant and business manager."

Amelia tensed. "When did this come about?"

"I guess she hasn't told you about what she discovered or when. It's her story to tell, but I took the job. It's going to be temporary. Just until she gets back from Europe. And once I get things back on track, I'll only be there parttime."

"What are you going to be doing?"

"Working with Ree," she said. "I know you don't believe me, but I don't really care. I've always worked my ass off for what I wanted just like my Daddy taught me. The woman I am right now, today, I'm good with her. Can you say the same?"

"What is that supposed to mean?" she demanded.

"Are you happy with the woman you are?"

"Not really, but you don't understand," she muttered. "I have—There are expectations, and I've been stupid or lazy or both." She clamped a hand over her mouth at the realization that part of the disaster that was her life was all her fault.

Ryan's hand on her thigh made her jump, and she shoved it off.

"I can't even pretend to understand your life Amelia," Ryan told her. "My Daddy was good to me. He'd have been proud of me if I'd a never gone to college or left this town. Long as I got a job and held it down, he wouldn't care if I was a ditchdigger. If I paid the bills and kept me happy, he'd be good with it."

"I guess my mother has similar expectations except college was always in my future, just like marrying a man of a certain class."

"A rich boy," Ryan said, a hardness to her tone. "Boy being the operative word."

"Yeah. She wants me to be a social climber who goes to a lot of parties and look down my nose at everyone not like me."

"Nothing bad in that if it's what you want or something you don't mind."

"I don't want that life," Amelia told her softly. "I'll lose my inheritance if I stay here."

"Are you close to your siblings? Your dad?"

"No. My dad left my mother when I was six. I haven't seen or heard from him. My stepdad never really liked me. I'm child three of three. My brother is like my mother and so is my sister."

"And you don't have a good relationship with either of your siblings?"

"No."

"That's sad," Ryan murmured as she took a turn. "Family is precious, but you seem to have a good relationship with Miss Genny."

"I always have," Amelia answered. "She's the one member of my family other than my grandfather that was nice."

"Nice?" Ryan laughed. "What does that mean?"

"It means not—" She broke off, and Ryan glanced over at her.

"Hey, sweetie, it's okay," she said giving Amelia's leg a brief squeeze. "Say no more."

"It's just my family is driven by money, position and power. My mother and grandmother can't seem to get enough of it. I think that's why my father left. I just don't understand why he didn't take me with him."

Chapter Six

"What are you doing to my daughter, Genny?" Felicia demanded. "She's refusing to come home this weekend."

"Hello, Felicia. How are you?"

"You need to send her home," she growled. "I don't want her down in that backwater town developing bad habits."

"What kind of habits do you think she's developing?"

"You think I haven't heard about you?" Felicia demanded in cold disdain. "I know you sneak around with a black man. I don't want my child getting in trouble and having to deal with a colossal mistake. I will not have a black grandchild."

She sighed. "Felicia, Amelia is a grown woman. She has a right to date whoever she wishes even if it's another woman, or God forbid, a black one, but I don't think a woman will be getting her pregnant."

"She doesn't have any right to make erroneous decisions that will make me look bad," Felicia snapped. "Now, you send her home to me and to Greg where she belongs."

"Greg Lorkin."

"He's Robert and Mariyam's son. He's a doctor, and he's damn good just like his father."

"I'm sure you know just how good his father is, but—"

"Just stop trying to take my daughter," Felicia cut in. "If you'd wanted one, you should have adopted one."

"Felicia, I don't care what you think of me," Genny replied coolly. "I'm certainly not going to tell Amelia how she can and cannot live her life. She has a right to be happy, but perhaps your reason for trying to marry her off is to gain control of her inheritance."

"I don't need her inheritance," Felicia replied coldly.

"Then, stop trying to control her."

"If she doesn't come home and do as I say, she's never getting her hands on her inheritance. It's that simple. Now, stay out of this," Felica snapped. "I'll come down there to get her if I have to."

"I think you should allow her the time she needs," Genny answered. "A year to decide if Greg Lorkin is what she wants—"

"I don't have to make deals with her," Felicia broke in angrily. "She has a duty to this family to marry the right man from the right family."

"What about her duty to herself?"

"I let her work at that school," she retorted. "She's had her chance to sow her wild oats. Now, I will be down there later in the week if I have to."

"That's what you're going to have to do," Genny replied.

"Do not mess with me Gen," Felicia warned her. "You might be older, but I'm smarter."

"No, Felicia, you just think you are," Genny answered.

Felicia was like her mother. Materialistic, thoughtless, and willing to use her influence to harm anyone who refused to bend to her will or get out of her way. She wasn't about to allow them to further imprison a lovely young woman whose spirit was starting to break under the weight of their cruelty.

"I always get what I want, Gen," she said softly. "Not even you can stop that so don't get in my way."

"Then, leave Amelia out of whatever games you and your mother are playing. She's not yours to give away." She ended the call and blew out a harsh breath. "That woman!"

"Amelia is the one who's going to have to stand up to her, Genny," Alston said from the other side of her desk. "I know you want to help her, but she's going to have to make a decision on her own now unless you're going to tell her about her father's heritage."

"I know," she said quietly. "No. I don't plan to do that without cause. I just hate to see her so unhappy. She used to be a vibrant girl, but Felicia slowly suffocated her." She shook her head and pushed away from the desk in her home office.

"You've given her a chance to break free and make a fresh start. The rest is up to her, and maybe hanging out with Hope and Kailey, she'll find the courage."

She grunted. "Ryan is interested in her."

He nodded slowly, a knowing look in his eyes. "I've noticed them noticing each other when they think no one is looking," he commented. "I've even seen them together having lunches at the inn."

"She could get hurt." She had noticed too, but she hadn't wanted to even think about Amelia getting involved with Ryan.

Ryan was a stone butch just like her two closest friends. She had a man's strength packed into her feminine body.

On top of that, Ryan wasn't all human and that within itself could be a problem since their world wasn't Amelia's. Likely never would be though she had hopes of bringing Amelia into her own coven.

"You know how rumors are," he replied with a hint of a smile. "Anyway, Ryan might be just what she needs. As I recall, you turned out to be exactly what I needed."

Genny smiled. "That's different. Amelia has been sheltered. I don't think she's ever had a real lover her entire life."

"Then, this could be just the nudge she needs to help her decide which world she wants to live in." Alston rose and rounded her desk. He kissed the top of her head.

"Amelia isn't the reason I asked you to come over." She caressed his arm as she stared up at him.

Her niece was important, had always been, that was why she'd kept in touch with Amelia over the years. However, business was her immediate concern.

"What is?" he asked, stopping in front of her.

"I have the full results of the audit, and I know who's been stealing from me. I'm going to go to the police."

"Do you have any proof?"

"Yes. Do you have anything from Aaron?" Aaron was the private detective she'd asked him to hire.

He nodded gravely. "You aren't going to like it."

****

Ryan pulled into the parking lot in the inn. On this side, they were close to the inn's small dock. They had a few small boats they used to bring in supplies as well as paddle boats that patrons could use for cruising the canal. However, it was only for patrons. Genny never opened the canal up to casual cruisers.

They climbed out, and Ryan grabbed a pack from the backseat of her dual cab pick-up. She slipped it on her back, and they headed to the dock and a thin man came out of the boat house.

"Hey, Ryan," he said. "Hello Miss Rose-Brier."

"Hey, Ty," Ryan answered. "Amelia Ty works here. He handles fishing and the boats."

"Oh. Nice to meet you," Amelia said.

"Miss Genny gave us permission to take a paddle boat out."

"Just sign and it's all yours," he replied.

"Charlie's joining us," Ryan told him.

"Fine by me," he said. "Come on in and put your John Hancock down."

She followed him into the boathouse, but Amelia waited for them outside.

"I've never actually met her," he murmured. "Miss Genny been keeping her locked up seems like."

"Naw," Ryan said waving him off. "She's a little shy. She doesn't get out much, but I think that's about to change."

"Oh, yeah?" he asked with raised brows.

She didn't reply as she scribbled her name and straightened.

"The girl's a bit innocent for your games," he said.

"Get a life, Ty," she replied.

"Hey, hey."

Ryan glanced to the door to find her old friend Charlie there. Glancing past her, she saw the golden-haired Hope who was talking to Amelia.

"Ty," Charlie said coolly.

"Charlie." He gave her a nod.

"We get the boat?"

"Yep."

"Take the one with the canopy," Ty said. "If I'm not here when you get back, you know what to do."

"Thanks," Ryan said. Ryan exited the structure with Charlie. "I see you brought Hope."

"I see you brought the snob," she said in a teasing tone. How's Miss Genny handling it?" They both stared to where the other two women stood, and Ryan noticed how comfortable Amelia looked talking to Hope.

"The best she can," Ryan said. "Anyway, like I told her, it's Amelia's word that matters."

"I bet she's not taking that well."

Ryan frowned. "What makes you think that?" Her gaze slid over Amelia slowly eating her up from her shapely pale legs to her pretty face.

"Hope says she thinks Amelia's family might not approve of the fact she's gay and makes it hard for her."

"Well, Amelia's choice to make," Ryan replied.

"I thought you were looking to settle down," Charlie said. "She's not one of us, Ryan. Are you going to keep that from her?"

Ryan shrugged. "I don't know what's going on, Charlie," she murmured. "I just know the very smell of her, the way she smiles has me in a vice grip."

"Could be the vampire's found her mate," Charlie commented. "I feel the same about Hope, but I'm not jumping in feet first."

Ryan laughed. "It's not the same. Hope is part of Thistle-Rose. She's one of us."

"You're kidding?" Charlie asked in a hushed tone.

"Think about it, Char," Ryan said and slapped her on the arm lightly. "She was at the Lupercalia Ball and not with a date."

"No, I thought she was with Annie."

"Yeah. That was over. Annie's such an ass. Hope is too good for that."

Charlie shrugged. "Genny's the house queen, maybe Amelia's actually one of us too."

"Amelia's mother is Miss Genny's half-sister, but Miss Genny's mother was one of us not her father."

"Do you know who Amelia's father is?" Charlie asked. "Miss Genny can't have kids, so maybe she hooked one of her coven members up with her sister to breed her an heir."

Ryan nodded slowly. "That could happen."

"Often does," Charlie said with a shrug.

"Yeah. The thing with Amelia is just—It's already complicated, but not today. Come on. Let's go enjoy the company of those lovely ladies."

Charlie grinned and slapped her on the back before starting forward.

Ryan followed, lightness in her soul.

Chapter Seven

Amelia watched as Ryan untied the boat and Charlie checked things out. She had no idea what she was doing, but she was going to learn.

She wasn't leaving this town. She was going to learn everything about the business and make herself in dispensable to her aunt, so she'd never want to let her go.

As for Ryan, Amelia wanted to learn everything about the woman who was captivating her more every day. Whether this became a love affair, or a fling didn't matter.

It was time she took responsibility for the life she wanted and stopped blaming her mother, her grandmother, and her inheritance. She could live free or die enslaved.

"What are you doing, Charlie?" Amelia asked curiously.

"Checking to make sure there's nothing wrong with the boat. The plug is obviously in, but I wanted to make sure it's in tight, and we're not taking on even the slightest bit of water. Also, I need to make sure the canopy is okay, and the pedals are working, and the wheel isn't sticking."

"But we won't know for sure until we go to turn it," Ryan said getting in and storing her pack in a compartment. "You want to learn about the boats?"

"I do," she said with a nod. "I want to learn everything about the business including how often my aunt allows the boats to be taken out."

"Talk to Ty. He'll know," Hope said. "And if you really want to learn more, you should spend some time with Addy. She's been manager for years."

"I'll do that," she said.

"Let's put out then," Charlie said sitting down next to Hope in the front of the boat that could easily seat six.

"We're peddling?" Amelia asked.

"Exactly, we're the power," Ryan told her giving her a wink. "When it comes time to turn, we'll let you know. We'll do all the work this trip. Next time I'll let you take the wheel."

"I'll be looking forward to it," Amelia said giving her a smile.

They peddled the boat out onto the canal, and Amelia was so caught up in the view that she stopped peddling at all. She wished she'd brought her camera, then she remembered she had her phone and pulled it from her pocket and began taking pictures.

They pulled to a stop next to a dock, and Ryan and Charlie climbed out to secure the boat. Then, Ryan grabbed her pack.

"Come on, sweetheart," Ryan said, extending a hand to her. "Let's have a little bit of a walk."

Amelia took it, and their eyes met. Heat washed over her, and something in Ryan's copper depths drew her in. It was like falling, and Amelia knew the water was deep.

Ryan's thumbed stroked the back of her hand and Amelia drew in a breath, the sensation of her touch made her sway a little even as her stomach clenched from the butterflies that fluttered in it.

Ryan tugged and Amelia allowed the momentum to carry her forward and right into Ryan who steadied her with a hand on her hip. Ryan's stare was warm, inviting.

"If we don't hook up with you guys, meet back here in thirty," Charlie said.

"Sure," Ryan answered not taking her eyes from Amelia, and Charlie and Hope started out ahead without them.

Heart beating fast, Amelia continued to hold Ryan's gaze. "You said you had no problem giving me the girlfriend experience," Amelia said quietly before her courage dissipated leaving her to second-guess herself later.

Ryan laughed. "Oh, that's what I agreed to, did I?"

"It was," she said shyly.

"So, that's why you're practically in my arms," Ryan teased, her copper gaze dancing with humor.

Amelia grinned. "I didn't know it was a crime to be so close to my girlfriend."

Ryan slipped an arm around her waist and drew her in closer. "Not at all." Her lips touched hers, and Amelia's breath hitched.

"You smell good," Ryan murmured and when she opened her mouth to reply, Ryan kissed her.

Amelia put her hand on Ryan's arm allowing herself to enjoy the moment despite that tightening in her stomach that came from years of always being on guard.

"And you're a good kisser," Ryan said.

Amelia smiled faintly, fingers lightly stroking Ryan's arm. "Why aren't you dating anyone? You seem nice enough."

Ryan shrugged. "What do you mean?"

"You know what I mean. Why aren't you in a relationship?"

Ryan's stare became shuddered now, and Amelia kicked herself for ruining the mood. "Why aren't you?"

"You know why," Amelia returned. "I guess you aren't interested in anything serious."

"No. I am," Ryan answered after a long beat of her heart. "I just haven't met anyone I want to attempt to build something special with."

"I hope spending time with me isn't going to be a problem," Amelia said. "I mean, you could be dating someone who might become special to you."

"You could," Ryan commented, and Amelia looked away. Ryan tightened her fingers on Amelia's slightly, and she looked at her. "I know you're not promising anything, so there's no need to climb into your shell."

"I wasn't," she said quietly.

She was afraid. Hopeful. Ryan was thinking the same thing about her she was thinking about her.

"Don't tell me you're still thinking I used you to get your aunt to hire me."

"No. I believe you about that. Have you met the accountant, Leah?"

"I know Leah. She's Addy's, the inn's manager, older sister."

"I didn't know. Did they grow up here?"

"Their parents died when Addy was fourteen, and she and Leah came to live with their aunt Dolly Hopewell. Dolly died five years ago."

"Did she and my aunt get along?"

"Not really." Amelia frowned. "Dolly's sister and Miss Genny used to be friends. They had a falling out, and Miss Genny and Dolly never got back on good terms."

"Why not?"

"There was lots of speculation Dolly was pissed off at Miss Genny over how things went between Dolly's sister, Delia and your aunt. Delia and your aunt were supposedly in a love triangle over your aunt's husband."

"Was it true?"

"Which part?" Ryan asked taking them deeper into the park.

"Any of it. All of it."

Ryan shrugged. "I don't know. I wasn't a fly on a wall when they were alone together."

"But?"

"But you should ask your aunt. Her life wasn't always what it is now. Plus, the fact she has more money than most people in this town especially Dolly and Delia played a part in their squabbles."

"Meaning?"

"Meaning, it wasn't public knowledge and if you want to know ask her."

"She and Alston are lovers." Amelia could tell just by looking at them. Alston was protective, thoughtful and kind to her aunt. He brought her little gifts too sometimes.

"I don't know. It's supposed, but only they know what goes on when they're alone."

"But your guess is?"

"I think they are and have been for a long time, but it's not my business."

"I can tell he cares about her," Amelia murmured. The raw energy and heat just rolled off them every time they were in the same room. It made her realize what she'd been missing from her own life. "He comes over for dinner every Tuesday, and she goes out to the city every Friday."

"Except when we're having events in town," Ryan said with a laugh. "Why do you care?"

"I saw something once when I was here. I was a kid," Amelia answered.

"What did you see?"

"I'm not sure. I was young. My memories could be off base."

"Tell me," Ryan urged gently.

"I was nine. There was a party at the inn."

"Was it summer?"

"Yes."

"Mid-Summer. There is a private ball every year. Well, three or four times a year. They're centered around some old vampire books. It's a very closed culture, and the invitees dress up like characters from the books."

"Wait. Are you saying my aunt thinks she's a vampire?"

"I'm saying she went to the ball. The characters in the books are witches and vampires," Ryan answered. "What happened, your memory?"

"I saw my aunt having sex with a guy in a mask, but I also saw my uncle with a woman in a mask."

Ryan shrugged. "They could have been swinging. It's encouraged at that ball as well as the Lupercalia and Beltane balls."

"Lupercalia?"

"An old Roman version of Valentine's day."

"Oh. Cool." She frowned. "My uncle didn't come home that night," she said. "I mean the man who carried me to my room wasn't him."

"Who was it?"

"The man my aunt was with."

Ryan shrugged again. "You could have been mistaken."

"I heard them talking. She was upset that my uncle wasn't coming home. She said she knew he was with that woman again. The guy tried to assure her that he wasn't cheating on her."

"Alston was your uncle's best friend," Ryan said. "Don't dwell on the past, their past. I don't think they do."

Amelia stumbled and Ryan caught her. Amelia looked up at her, their gazes held. Her breath came out in a whoosh at the heat in Ryan's stare. Her heart thudded and her skin heated.

"Okay?" Ryan asked.

"Yeah," she said breathlessly and looked away.

This was—it was intense. It was unlike any other crush she'd ever had.

"Let's head that way," Ryan said. "We can get a good look at the lake and the inn from there."

Amelia allowed Ryan to navigate the way over the sloping terrain. The trees shielded them from the sun which had grown hotter. They reached the top of the hill and tall trees provided even more shade.

"Water?" Ryan asked taking her pack off her back.

"Please."

Ryan handed her an insulated bottle and produced one for herself.

Amelia took a drink and studied the view. "It's really beautiful," she said.

"Yeah, it is," Ryan murmured, and Amelia looked at her to find Ryan studying her.

"Is your skin okay? I have a hat."

"I probably better take it," Amelia said.

Ryan gave her the wide brimmed white hat, and Amelia handed over her bottle and took the hat. She put it on, thankful, because she knew she'd start to burn on the way back down.

That was one of the drawbacks of being a redhead with pale skin.

"Thanks," she said after putting the hat on. "I normally think of things like this myself."

"Well, it's a girlfriend's prerogative to be thoughtful."

Amelia laughed. "You aren't going to let me live that down, are you?"

"No way, girlfriend," she said and put an arm around her waist. "Come on, there's another view I want you to see."

Ryan led her further up the hill to a grove of trees, and Amelia stopped, and her jaw dropped on seeing the landscape dotted by cherry red blooms.

"Oh my god," she gasped. "Beautiful."

"Dynamic crape myrtle," Ryan murmured. "They bloom until the first frost and start to die off."

"I need one of these down at the inn."

"Then, we'll find you one," Ryan told her.

"Within budget of course," Amelia said making a face.

"As my girlfriend, you probably could find a way to convince me to get you one as a gift," Ryan teased.

"Hmm," Amelia said. "Why didn't I think of that?"

Ryan chuckled. "I guess because you're new at all this girlfriend stuff."

"That could be it," Amelia said leaning toward her and staring up into her eyes.

"You have beautiful eyes," Ryan said softly.

"I was just thinking the same about you."

Ryan dipped her head and their lips met in a soft kiss. Amelia braced a hand on Ryan's arm. Ryan's skin was soft and drew her in, making her want to cuddle closer, but she restrained herself.

Ryan wrapped an arm around Amelia's waist and just held her for a moment, their lips touching. The warmth of Ryan, the scent of her, was sublime, and the moment was perfect in its simplicity.

Chapter Eight

After dropping Amelia off, Ryan headed for the old Victorian her father had converted into a home for his small covenant. There had only been twenty of them, all night walkers just like him.

Ryan often wondered how her mother had been seduced by a vampire, but then she remembered how kind he'd been to her.

There had been something about him that had made it so hard not to like him. She knew it was in part due to the vampire mystique. The other part had been just who he was.

She wondered what Uncle Mihai was going to ask or tell her about Amelia. Ryan also wondered what was it that had brought him back here. Mihai hadn't been in town since the summer she left for college. She'd seen him that night and after that he was gone.

The house wasn't far from where she lived so it only took her five more minutes to get to the house than it would take to get to her own.

Ryan parked in the driveway and went inside. She stopped short at the sight of the butler in the corridor. The brown-haired man inclined his head to her.

He was a human who'd aged well over the years making Amelia wonder if her uncle had finally brought him across, made him a vampire.

"Ryan," he said. "I'll go and tell your uncle that you're here."

"Thank you," she answered.

She went into the foyer and waited for him to return. When he did, he gave her a nod.

"Would you like some tea?"

"No, thanks," she answered.

"You can go right up," he told her.

Ryan took the stairs up to his suite of rooms. He sat in a chair, the room dimly lit, and the windows heavily shielded against the early fall sunlight. His hair, dark brown, was longer than the last time she'd seen him, and he was clad in slacks and a shirt with a vest.

Mihai rose and came to greet her, hugging her. "Hello, my dear."

"Hello, Uncle Mihai." She kissed his cheek. "You look fit." He was thin with paler skin than normal. His gray eyes regarded her warmly.

"You have a glow about you," he said, surveying her as he backed to the chair in the spacious room. With a hand, he motioned to the sofa before which was a table with a pot on it. "I just had the tea brought up."

"No," she said. "I'm going to a gathering with friends."

"Your coven?" he asked.

The vampires often referred to their families as houses, clans, or covens. The Vampire Council was a world-wide body that set forth certain rules, but each coven, clan, or house was an autonomous unit with their own elder, elders or court.

The court consisted of a vampire king or queen and a court of elders which were sometimes called dukes and duchesses. To be a king or queen, one had to have sired several vampires or have been born the offspring of a king or queen who had been killed.

Like in human royalty, the king or queen's offspring were called princes or princesses. They could take over the house, coven, or clan at their parent's death if they desired or unless the elders rose against them and prevented it.

Those of the culture adhered to the set rules to protect the species from the hunters, humans, who often destroyed entire covens when possible.

"Yes."

"The Council here wants the House of Knight to once again take its place among the hierarchy," he told her.

"What does that mean?" She had been raised by a human. That she had been born of a vampire king had given her rank and title that she had seen as more or less useless.

"It means, you're to be acknowledged as your father's daughter, and you're expected to take his place here in this town."

"In what capacity?" she asked with a frown.

"You're to participate in the vampire culture and take your place in the town's Council of Elders."

She drew in a breath and let it out slowly as she studied him. Ryan had never thought being part of the House of Knight would ever mean fully interacting with other vampires in the area.

She never had before.

They left her on her own, and she was glad for her family's sake. The sometimes petty squabbles could spill over onto her father and his family.

"Times change, Ryan," he told her. "The Council head is pushing for the organization here to be more active. I told him I would pass that along."

"Who is the head?" she asked.

"I think he said you knew him. His name is Jaxon Rider."

"I know Rider," she said with a smile. "He tried to pair me with his son."

"His mother is a witch like yours, but his father is no king."

"His son is no prize. He's a screw up with no ambition or follow through."

He smiled. "As your father's heir you are expected to take over the House of Knight and produce at least one heir."

"How am I supposed to do that? I'm not a man, and I'm not about to get pregnant."

"By marrying a woman who gives birth to a child with your family's blood. There are some humans of the bloodline left who I've managed to secure material from."

"Why did you do that?"

"Your father asked me to. I'm also here to do one other thing I was asked to do," he told her.

"What's that?"

"On the table is an envelope," he responded. "It's from your father."

"Why is the council seeking to become more active now?" Ryan was curious.

"There is talk some of the old ones here are going to have to leave. They don't want the vampire culture or presence to die leaving the territory open to newer vampires with less civilized codes of conduct."

"Do they have a reason to be concerned about that?" she asked. "I haven't heard of or noticed any unexplained deaths."

"You'd have to talk to Rider," he told her.

Ryan nodded, picking up the envelope and opened it. She knew her father's handwriting thanks to a series of letters he'd written to her mother. Her mother had saved them, and Ryan had inherited them along with a few of her mother's things.

She had gotten to know him better through those letters. The relationship between him and her mother had been one of soul touching love that she hoped to find one day.

Ryan read the letter. It was two pages of neatly written words. It was direction, advice, and acknowledgement of her as a child he'd loved and wanted.

"Your father wanted you to have this house in the event you created your own coven but since you don't appear to be interested in that, you're free to sell this one if you like."

"I prefer to stay in my own home," she told him. "You can have it if you want it."

"Thank you," he answered. "Your father would be proud of you."

She gave him a smile. "You've prepared me well, Uncle Mihai," Ryan replied. She knew the culture well thanks to him. She knew what her father had built here and was ready to take over.

"I must tell you one more thing," he said.

"What is it?" she asked.

"The Rose you're seeing," he said.

"She's not. I told you, but I'm assuming you're referring to the vampire coven."

"Her father was a member of the Thistle-Rose coven. His family is modestly wealthy but is famous in the west. Thistle-Rose was founded by his family and Genny's. He was a member of the branch of the coven that resides here before marrying Genny's sister."

Her lips parted in a silent O.

"The marriage didn't last, but the girl's mother was human. However, I don't believe she's fully human. Her father had an amulet made for her because she was allergic to the sun. So, she's more vampire than human."

"Why wouldn't her father take her with him?"

"I don't know," he said. "At any rate, Rose-Briers had a genetic flaw in their genetics that made a few an anomaly."

"How so?"

"They survived not on blood but on energy," he replied quietly.

"Energy?"

"Energy is what feeds them. Some dark, some sexual, some both, but they still had the same vampiric issues as the rest of us. The sun. There are no day-walkers among their clan just as there were none in your father's until you."

Ryan frowned.

"They were still every bit the vampire, Ryan, every bit as dangerous as the rest of us," he told her. "So, don't think she's safer."

"I don't know what to think yet," she told him.

"Just be careful, they can drain those they feed from too," Mihai told her. "And they do feed just as we must."

"I see." Ryan answered.

"I'm not that versed in their feeding techniques, but I think they can use touch. Some have been known to bite, but it's a psychic tearing of the aura not a physical tearing. They are usually dormant until something awakens the vampire within."

"Something like what?" Ryan asked.

"A bite from a vampire, a werewolf, or even a wolf shifter."

Oh, no. She had bitten her last night.

"What will happen once they're awakened?" Ryan asked, breath held.

"No, they don't go insane, feeding from everyone they come into contact with," Mihai answered with a smile, his gray eyes dancing with humor. "Most of them are nowhere near as destructive as a newly turned vampire. They hunger, but they don't feed indiscriminately because it takes a few days or weeks for their hunger to become overpowering enough that they organically seek to feed it."

"They feed off energy instinctively?"

"Yes."

She sighed. She was going to have to learn as much as she could about energetic vampires so she could help Amelia through the change. If indeed Mihai was right.

"I have to leave tonight, but I'll return soon there is some business I have to take care of."

"Thanks," she said and got to her feet. "I'm running late, but I look forward to catching up with you on your next visit."

He rose and inclined his head. "I'll see you then, Ryan."

She smiled and hugged him and then left the house with a smile. Her father had been a good man, and a good leader of his people. Ryan didn't have a coven to lead, just her two friends. She didn't expect her life to be as extraordinary as his had been.

Royalty in life and then bitten by a vampire and turned, he'd been royalty as an undead. He'd sired over a hundred before helping to create her, his most beloved child.

But she would attempt to make him proud.

****

Genny heard Amelia return two hours after she'd left. She listened, waiting for her to come looking for her, but she didn't.

She glanced at her tablet and the changes she'd made. She had been glad to make them and hoped Amelia would become even half the caretaker she had been.

She would train her well and ensure she had at least one other person who would assist her in moving into the role as head of the coven. She hadn't thought Amelia would ever be here, but she had hoped. Now, she would have to make the moves that would keep her here.

She wasn't sure how she would do it yet. Bite her or allow someone else to, but her destiny was here in Avon Del.

However, she wouldn't force her to take the reins of her heritage should she refuse. Course for her to refuse, Genny had to tell her, and she was dragging her feet for fear Amelia wouldn't accept her place here.

Genny glanced back to her tablet. The file there had confirmed something she'd known for a very long time, but she'd allowed it to stay hidden thinking the past was just that.

Her husband had been a decent man in so many ways, but when his family had slowly gone broke, he'd become a bit bitter, and as she'd discovered, attempted to regain his own personal fortune by doing the unthinkable.

It had been unthinkable only because she'd cared for him and thought he at least respected her despite the man he'd become. He'd had trouble accepting the bad decisions he'd made and that she was the one with all the money and thus in his eyes, the power.

She had inherited this property on her eighteenth birthday, a valuable piece of land that had been in her mother's family for centuries. The land included what was now a park. They had developed Avon Del Park, each generation adding something to it.

The canal had been the reason they'd bought the land. In fact, her mother's family had been one of the three founding families who'd built this town to the place it was on their blood, sweat and tears.

"Aunt Genny," Amelia called, and she smiled. "Auntie?"

"I'm in the office," she called.

Amelia appeared in the open doorway a moment later.

"Did you have fun with the boys and Hope?" she asked. Ty had called her about the boat letting her know who was going out on it. That's how she knew Hope had been there.

"What do you mean, boys?" she asked moving further into the room.

She smiled. "Ryan and Charlie."

"Why do you call them boys?" she asked with a frown.

"Because they're quite tomboyish."

She frowned as she came to a stop before her desk. "What I saw of the park is beautiful," Amelia said. "I was wondering if you'd consider giving me a more permanent job."

Hope bloomed in her. "What about Greg Lorkin and your mother?"

"Nothing about them," Amelia replied with a shrug, her expression determined. "That's not my life, and I'm not going to be forced into it."

"What's brought this on?" Genny asked curiously. "Ryan?"

"She's part of it, I admit, but no." She shook her head. "I just think it's about time I took control of my life." She smiled, and Genny had to smile too.

There was a light in Amelia's eyes that she'd never seen. It radiated from the inside out giving Amelia a quiet strength. She would give Amelia any help she needed to help it grow.

"You'll need to learn the business more fully because you'll be in control of things while I'm gone. Not just the inn, but the financial part as well."

"I like a challenge," she said softly.

"Good because it won't be easy," Genny said.

"I think I can handle."

Of course, she could, she was a Thistle.

"You look pretty." She had on another dress Genny had never seen and her red hair, hair like Genny's grandmother's, was done in a casual updo that enhanced her beauty.

"I'm going to a barbecue with Ryan. Her friend Rena's."

"Ah." She nodded. "Have fun with the boys."

"I'll be moving to the guest house," she said. "Is that okay?"

"It's fine, but you're allowed to have guests here. We're both adults and you have an entire wing of the house to yourself. I'm not likely to hear you and Ryan."

"I don't want to do anything that will make you uncomfortable," Amelia said.

Genny laughed. "I don't have a problem with your sexuality." She doubted Amelia would bring Ryan home even if she gave her the guesthouse. She was too much of a good girl.

"If you're sure," she said looking uncertain.

"It's okay with me if you entertain Ryan. She's going to be working for me. Are you going to be okay with that?"

"Did she ask you for a job?"

"No. In fact, she initially refused when I offered. Her friend Ree is a financial banker, investor and does good business. She handles some investments for me. Ryan was going to work for her."

"You asked her not to?"

"Yes," Genny said. "Why do you ask?"

"I was curious."

"Ryan was a stockbroker herself. She was very good at it from what I've learned. I'll probably put her in charge of my account."

"You trust her?"

"She's given me no reason not to. Besides, I know her father. He's a good man, and I know he raised Ryan to be a good guy."

Amelia was about to speak when the doorbell rang. "That'll be Ryan. I'll see you later."

"Have fun."

"I think I will," she said and there was a confident look in her eyes as she turned and strode from the room.

Well, things were about to get interesting if Amelia was going to embrace her own power as a woman, a daughter of Thistle-Rose.

Chapter Nine

"Hi," Ryan said when Amelia opened the door for her. "You look fantastic."

Amelia gave her a shy smile. "Thank you."

The green blouse had a square neckline and tiny pearl buttons, and she'd paired it with a black wrap skirt and the wedge heels.

"I brought you something," Ryan said and reached into her pocket for the small box. She'd opted for this rather than flowers. It would last longer than flowers and maybe could be her first gift to the woman who stood next to her in months to come.

Amelia's eyes lit up. "Ryan," she said in a chastising tone, but it was clear she was pleased. That made Ryan wonder how often anyone thought of her, gave her anything just for her.

"I know. Dad always said take flowers on the first date, but I figured this would work just as well."

Amelia opened the small box and grinned. "Ryan!" She threw one arm around Ryan, and Ryan hugged her close, taking in the soft smell of her.

"It's beautiful. I'm going to put this on my necklace," Amelia said, pulling back.

The necklace appeared to be one of those signature charm types as well. The chain rested just above the valley of her breasts along with the faintest hint of something, the amulet. It appeared to be nothing more than a charm on the chain, but it was clear to Ryan that wasn't the case.

Witch magic would have created the amulet that was woven into her skin and could never be removed except by Amelia herself if she could even see it.

"Need some help?" Ryan purred.

"Yes." She turned and lifted the curtain of her red hair, and Ryan leaned in to unclasp the chain and found herself getting closer than necessary.

Amelia's perfume was provocative in its simplicity just like her outfit.

Just like Amelia.

She removed the necklace, and Amelia held the box out to her. "Will you?"

Ryan took it and watched as Amelia deftly removed one charm and replaced it with the rose she'd given her. Then, Amelia held the necklace out to Ryan who replaced it around her neck.

Unable to resist the temptation, Ryan kissed her nape, and Amelia faced her, her green eyes darkening.

"I love it," Amelia said. "Thank you. The rose will never lose its bloom, and I'll have the perfect memory of our first date preserved without trying to dry the rose."

"In that case, I made a good choice. Why don't we take a selfie?" Ryan pulled out her phone.

"Great idea," Amelia said. "Send it to me?"

"Naturally. You can't have the perfect memory without a picture."

She moved close to Amelia putting her arm around her and taking not one but three pictures of them.

"Is it prom night?"

"Aunt Genny," Amelia said.

"I know," Miss Genny said. "You two want that for your social media."

"That's a great idea," Amelia exclaimed. "Ryan, send the second one to me."

"You may as well change your status to in a relationship too," Ryan teased.

"I have to do that," Amelia agreed giving her a wicked grin.

"Uh, what?" Miss Genny asked, a confused look on her face. "When did all this happen? You spend an evening looking at the stars and an afternoon on the water, and you're in a relationship?"

"Aunt Genny, this is older than that," Amelia said in a chastising tone, giving Ryan a conspiratorial look.

"Oh, yeah, Miss Genny. It's at least a couple of weeks—"

"Ryan," Amelia said in a chastising tone. "Look what Ryan got me for our four-week anniversary." Amelia lifted the charm.

Ryan fought back laughter. Four weeks ago, Amelia had served her at the inn's restaurant, and they'd flirted a little. That's when Ryan knew she'd ask Amelia out if she got the chance. Friday the door had swung wide open.

"Four weeks?" Miss Genny asked carefully and slanted a look at Ryan. The doubt in her blue eyes was overtaken by disbelief. "Ryan?"

"Auntie," Amelia said moving to stand next to Ryan. "Ryan, will you keep this for me?"

Ryan took the A charm from Amelia and slipped it into her pants pocket.

"Thanks. Should we go?" Amelia asked. "Auntie, we'll see you later."

Miss Genny gave Ryan a curious look. "Why didn't you tell me you two were dating?"

"Because I asked her not to," Amelia said slipping an arm around Ryan. "I didn't want to upset you, but now that I know you're okay with it, it's fine if people know."

"Do people include your mother?" Miss Genny asked.

"She'll find out soon enough," Amelia replied airily. "I won't be hiding it." She went on tip toe and kissed Ryan. "See you later." Amelia headed for the door.

"Ryan," Miss Genny growled. "What in the hell is going on? Is this some fauxmance as you kids call it?"

"Not really," she said.

"Ryan?" Amelia called.

"We'll talk about this later," Miss Genny muttered. "And I want the truth, Ryan Baptist."

"You'll have it," Ryan assured her and followed Amelia out the door.

They made their way to Ryan's truck in the driveway, and Ryan pulled open the door for her, and Amelia got in. Ryan got in on her side and started the truck.

"Are you going to tell her that we haven't been dating?"

"I can tell her whatever you want me to," Ryan replied. "I just wonder why you'd want to lie to her."

"I sort of told my sister I was seeing someone. She called me to do my mother's bidding again. I told her I wasn't coming home because I was seeing someone."

Ryan nodded. "Okay, so what happens if she comes down here to drag you home?"

"Grace? Oh, she's not coming down here. This small town is beneath her. She married the son of a big toy company. They pull in millions a year. She loves everything Avon Del isn't."

"The city," Ryan surmised. Avon Del wasn't the city, but they did have a few things going for them.

Good shopping, a small theatre, minor league ball club, a nice museum, the community college, and the park. They also had a myriad of activities including the new ice rink for winter. The rink was a joint project that was funded by the local business association and the kids had just gotten a hockey league to offset some of the maintenance costs.

Amelia put her hand on Ryan's thigh and her muscles tensed even as sensation rippled through her.

"Please? I need people to think we're dating. You said you'd be willing to be my secret lover."

"Are you sure you want to go down that road of pretend?"

"I don't understand. I thought we were sort of dating."

Ryan laughed. "We did agree to that in a roundabout way, but I meant the pretending we've been dating longer."

"If you don't want to, I understand."

"I have no problems helping you," Ryan told her. "You're too pretty to say no to, but why would you want to play pretend?"

"I know where I want my life to go, Ryan, and it's not in the direction of a marriage to a man I'll never love. I don't even know why he's agreeing to this. I've only let him kiss me once."

"I see."

"He made moves, and I rebuffed at every turn."

"Your inheritance is dependent on you marrying him?"

"Yes, and I'm saying screw it. I'd rather be happy than trapped. I want more of what we did today. I want you. I don't know if it's just a crush, but I'd like to find out."

"Am—"

"I don't want to hide to do it. I don't care who knows."

Ryan nodded. "Sounds like a plan."

Ryan was more than a little attracted to the red-headed beauty who didn't even seem to know how pretty and desirable she was.

Her thoughts slid quickly from solitary reverie as Amelia's hand moved inward on her thigh. Ryan had strapped up tonight in anticipation, but she had no intentions of pushing.

"Bad girl," Ryan drawled putting her hand on Amelia's as it drifted even closer toward her crotch.

"I—Sorry," she said quickly jerking her hand back.

Ryan laughed. "I don't mind you getting personal, but it seems to me you're just fishing."

"What do you mean?" Amelia asked nervously.

"I think you want to know if I'm really wearing a strap-on. Yeah. I am and yeah, I wear it often. I don't think I'm a guy or even want to be one, but sex can be so much fun with a toy."

"I've never—I mean I want to try that too."

Ryan grinned. "Good to hear," she murmured. "Because I'd love to show you how it works." Ryan glanced over at her and recalled how close Amelia stood to her at times.

She was touch starved. Amelia just needed human contact. She needed to feel desired, cared for.

That could make things interesting, or it could be incredible as the vampire Amelia was fully emerged.

"Give me your hand," Ryan said.

Amelia did just that, and Ryan put Amelia's hand on her thigh.

"Charlie seemed nice," Amelia said relaxing her fingers against the firmness of Ryan's thigh.

"She's a great woman."

"Why didn't she go to New York with you and Ree?"

"She couldn't see herself making a life anywhere but here," Ryan answered. "Plus, she has a younger brother that she had to raise. Her parents died. He's at LSU now."

"She gave up her life," Amelia murmured.

"Part of it." She shrugged.

She and Ree had sent money back to help with the hard times. When Charlie had come to visit them in New York, she'd brought her brother and Ryan and Ree had footed the bill for their stay just as they'd pulled together to help him go to college.

Naturally, Ryan's father had helped look out for him here providing a father figure.

"That was kind of her."

"That's what family does, Amelia." She put her hand on Amelia's briefly.

"Did we need to bring something? I forgot—"

"I got it," Ryan broke in. "Dessert."

"Okay. Great."

"Relax, Amelia," Ryan said and squeezed her fingers. "They just want to get to know you."

"I'm just nervous. It's been a long time since I've hung out with anyone other than women my mother said were appropriate."

"I guess we'd be on the hell no list," Ryan said with a grin.

"Definitely."

"It'll be fine. Trust me."

Course it would be fine. Her friends wouldn't judge Amelia, and they certainly wouldn't do it to her face. They would treat her with the same kindness they'd treat any newcomer who hadn't done anything to hurt them.

So, it was going to be a nice evening.

Chapter Ten

"Oh, god," Alston groaned as he stared up at her. His brown eyes were vivid pools of desire in his light-gold skin.

His fingers gripped her hips, nails biting into her as he sat up. Genny rocked on the thick cock inside her, and her body pulled tight as her orgasm washed over her. Then, the sharp prick at the side of her neck threw her into a second orgasm giving her that same electric feeling of invincibility she always got from making love with him.

He took a deep pull from her, and she closed her eyes, her fingers lightly stroking his chest. After he'd drank his fill, Alston lay back, breathing shallow.

Genny panted, sated, as the tension eased, and she continued to sit astride him, hands on his chest covering the mark that had been burned into his flesh so many years ago.

She had a similar one on her upper arm where the fire opal and clear quartz she'd been given as a child had burned her own skin.

"Al, I swear you'll still be making me hot in ten years," Genny murmured and leaned down to kiss him. She didn't need to feed as she'd already done so. The blood she'd consumed still lived inside her, his for the tasting.

His arms came around her making her feel warm and safe. This man had her. He'd stolen her heart slowly with his tenderness, his loyalty and his care for her. His love had come quietly, so quietly, she'd almost missed it.

Now, Genny had no plans to let him go.

"I love you too, Gen," he panted out. "More than you'll ever know."

She straightened and caressed his cheek. "Probably," she agreed softly and climbed off him and then got out of bed to pad into the bathroom.

Genny lifted the lid of the toilet seat and peed. Then, she washed up and cleaned the sticky essence from her. He hadn't used a condom, but then she couldn't have children, so it didn't matter.

"What are you thinking, beautiful?" he asked moving into the bathroom behind her.

She met his gaze in the mirror as he moved behind her.

"Amelia asked me to hire her permanently."

"I thought that was your plan, to give her a home here," he said with a frown.

"I know I've made plans for her future, but they all include her consent."

"I think she'll stay," he said and kissed her shoulder. "I also think that crush on Ryan is something more."

"She said she's been seeing her for four weeks." Genny shook her head and faced him leaning her backside against the counter.

"Maybe she has," he said with a shrug. "Could be longer for all you know. They've been seen chatting briefly at the farmer's market, dining together in the inn's dining room, and flirting. Remember that night you said she was sneaking back in?"

"I remember," she said with a frown. She just didn't want to believe it. Amelia had never been that kind of deceptive girl.

He grinned. "She hasn't openly lied, has she? I mean, have you asked her if she was seeing someone?"

"No. I just assumed she'd been taking a walk."

"She could have been coming back from a walk with Ryan. Ryan isn't a bad kid you know. Her stepfather did a good job with her. Granted he raised her more like she was a boy."

She smiled faintly. Ryan had been the perfect athlete and a great student graduating a year early along with her two friends. Ryan had been second in her graduating class and third in her graduating college class.

"You have to admit," he said breaking into her thoughts. "Ryan is the perfect mate for Amelia. She's strong, more dominant, intelligent, capable, and I think she'd be supportive of her as she grows more firmly into the woman she could be."

Genny nodded in agreement. Ryan could be to Amelia what Alston had been to her and look at them. Their love story was ever evolving, ever strengthening. It had started with a few stolen moments in the moonlight one summer.

But she had known him since she was seventeen. They had both had a love for the same subculture that some believed had grown out of some goth tales of a sexy vampire and her witch best friend.

The people of Avon Del would never know. Her husband certainly hadn't seen what was right under his nose.

"Let's hope what's happening is real."

"No. I hope Amelia has the courage to go after what she wants."

"Ryan and the girls are being invited to join," Alston murmured caressing her low back. "She carries the mark."

"It didn't come from her mother," Genny said softly thinking of Ryan's mother, the hoodoo witch from New Orleans.

She had been a lovely woman and the man who'd given her Ryan had been one of the night walkers. Dark and mysterious, the founder of a small coven that had only three members today where there had once been thirty.

"I know." He sighed. "None of them did, but the council agrees its time to acknowledge his coven."

"Are they sure?" she asked. True blood vampires were rare, the covens small especially here in the South where the sun could be so bright for so many months of the year. Here in Avon Del, though, three covens had made their home, two with Queens from founding families.

Ryan's father had been a vampire king, who'd brought his own covenant with him and settled in the eastern most part of the town.

He'd been from Romania and could do what none of them could, shift into a wolf as well as a bat.

"Yes," Alston answered. "She is Knight's daughter."

"She walks in the light," she murmured. "How?"

"She was born of a woman, a woman of light. A human, unlike us. Only the amulets allow us to walk in the light," he murmured stroking her hip. "There is talk that she will take his name for use only in our circles."

That was a big deal. The vampire courts, especially those of night, the nightwalkers, had kept to the old ways of a royal court and its disciples. So, old bloodlines, old family names carried more weight here than newly made or daywalkers.

Her mother had been a duchess of the court of Thistle-Rose, the first true vampire court in the area. She bore that title now and was in their circle the Grand Duchess of North, so called for the area of town where she lived. This was her territory which so happened to extend as far as the park did into two other towns giving her the biggest share in the area.

"When?"

"At the Yule ball," he said. "You know you have to tell her if she's staying. Her life, her world as your heir, as a Rose-Brier will be affected."

She nodded tightly. The Vampire Council had asked a favor of her that she had agreed to.

Therefore, she couldn't leave her territory unprotected which she was virtually doing despite having her heir here. She had to tie Amelia to someone with power. Ryan could be that someone.

Ryan hadn't participated in the Council, but she would be a sitting member if she took her father's vacant seat. The seat had been held temporarily by an Elder of Knight. With that Elder leaving the area for good, it was time the true heir took his seat.

"Has Amelia shown any signs?" Alston asked pulling her from her thoughts.

"No, but there is something different about her energy," Genny murmured. "She smells different."

"That could just be the scent of the wolf," he replied carefully. "I've heard stories of Mihai running with a young wolf."

"Ryan."

He nodded. "More than likely. When she was young, she had those ice blue eyes that he used to get when he went wolf," Alston told her. "It's been said her eyes change when she's upset."

"I've heard that too." She'd never seen it and as far as she knew no one had seen that in Ryan once she became a teenager.

She was either in great control of her animal or the ability to shift into the wolf had left her.

"Ryan could have woken the vampire in her. She'll need to feed soon," Alston replied gently. "She'll need to know what's happening to her."

"It won't happen right away. She'll fight it at first."

"Honey, you can't wait too long. The Council won't be happy with you if she kills someone. However, her connection with Ryan could be exactly what she needs right now. Ryan is sure to notice the signs of a hungry vampire and feed her."

"I don't want Ryan being her teacher."

"She's not her sire, just a peer, a lover who can teach her the ways of our world. Besides that, a connection with the House of Knight could join to powerful families."

"I know, but I won't force—" Her phone rang, and she sighed. She would never force the union. That would be up to Amelia's father, and if Amelia did change, he would have to be notified.

"I can't imagine who that could be, but—" His phone rang too, and he smiled.

"I'll be glad to leave this behind for France," Alston told her and followed her from the bathroom to the bedroom.

She picked up her phone. "Yes?"

"Hello Aunt Genevieve."

"Grace?" she asked. "What's wrong? Is Felicia okay?"

"Oh, yes. Mother is fine," she said, her tone holding a hint of a crisp edge. "I was just calling to find out if you were home or if you could have your houseman let me in."

"Let you in?" she asked with raised brows even as she tensed.

"I'll be there by seven tonight. Mother sent me to talks some sense into Amelia and to remind her of her place."

"I see," she said. "Well, I'm home now, but I'm going out for the evening, but I'll have Terra let you in and get a room ready for you."

"Thank you. I'll require a light meal."

"I'll have something prepared," Genny replied. "Grace, are you coming alone?"

"No. Victor is coming with me, but Anne will be staying in the city. I won't subject her to that town the way my mother subjected me to it. But Victor and I will be staying a few days."

"You might be more comfortable at the inn then," she said thinking of Amelia's announced plans for later this evening.

Then again, now would be the perfect time for Amelia to confront what would come if she chose to defy her mother.

"Actually, I'd prefer to stay at your home if that's possible," Grace said. "But if you don't want me there with Victor—"

"No. You're a grown and married woman. I wouldn't dream of excluding your husband."

"Perfect then," Grace said cheerfully. "Could you let Amelia know I'd like her to join us for dinner?"

"She's having an early dinner out," Genny told her. "But I'll leave word for her that you'd like her to join you two for dessert or coffee."

"I'll appreciate that," she said. "Dining out?"

"She's at a gathering with friends."

"Oh. I'll see her tonight. We do have much to discuss. I'll talk to you later too."

"I'll see you later, Grace." She hit end and shook her head. Why send Grace?

The two girls hadn't been close in years. Grace had adored her younger sister once upon a time, but they had slowly drifted apart.

"That was Barrett," Alston said mentioning his son. "The detective has confirmed his preliminary findings. Do you want to move ahead?"

"Yes." She nodded grimly. "I don't know what the motivation could have been, but I paid my dues years ago."

"You owed no debt on that score," he said.

"I know." She blew out a harsh breath. "I know."

No. She'd put the issue to bed years ago and had considered it a sleeping baby. It was a surprise to find she was wrong.

Chapter Eleven

"Hi, Amelia," Elise said warmly and gave her a hug. "You look hot in that outfit." She took her hand and led her across the patio. "Ree loves to grill, and my job is potato salad, green salad or macaroni salad. Today I made twice bake potatoes and a green salad. Is that okay? I can make you something else."

"No. That's fine," she said.

"Great. Sit down. Ree and Ryan will be huddled at the grill talking shop until Charlie gets here. Then, they'll come out of it for a bit. After that, it'll be sports talk and maybe an impromptu basketball game."

"Sounds like they leave you out." She glanced to where Ryan and Ree were laughing at the grill now. Ree held a plate, and Ryan was checking what was already on it.

"Not in the least." She shook her head. "I don't play ball with them, but I can hold my own in a conversation even if that's by changing it."

"You must strange just being you," Amelia said glancing back to Ryan and Ree. The parties with her family and their friends were never like that.

Ryan looked over then and their gazes held for a moment before she looked away.

"I manage. So, you and Ryan are hanging out?"

"We've been seeing each other," she said before she could stop herself. "A few weeks."

Elise nodded. "Secret lovers, huh? Well, go you. I didn't think you had it in you, but I should have guessed. Ryan's so protective of you. I told Ryan I was going to invite you over last weekend for a bit of fun, sex fun." She grinned. "Ryan said to leave you alone. Should have known she was saving you for herself."

"A menage?"

Elise gave her a wicked look. "I wanted one last fling, but alas that wasn't to be."

"What do you mean?"

"Ree and I are going off menages and swinging. We've both decided it was time to get serious and think about building something more lasting. We both want kids, and she doesn't want to bring a kid into that kind of a relationship."

"It might be hard on them."

"Maybe. But I'm committed to giving it a try," she said with a shrug. "I don't know if I can live that way forever."

"Why not? If you love Rena, then—"

"Love is love, but—" She shook her head. "I doubt you'll be wrestling with that question, and I know Ryan won't. She stopped fooling around with us so long ago. So did Charlie who was never into it anyway."

"Me either."

Elise put her hand on Amelia's. "You shouldn't knock it until you've tried it. There is nothing as seductive as two or even three women focused primarily on you."

"I guess it could have its charms."

Elise smiled. "Maybe you'll find out soon."

****

"Have you heard anything about anything that might make the Council want all covens on deck?" Ryan asked.

"I heard that some of the elders in a few covens are leaving," Ree told her with a shrug. "It's time for them to move on because of their age."

"I figured that," she said. "It's why Mihai hasn't been around. He told me the Council wanted the House of Knight back in the mix."

"I guess so," Ree murmured. "You grew up here, know the area, plus you're a master's heir."

Ryan shrugged. She was her father's child in some respects. She could shape shift as he could, her ability to bend light was incredible though she had found no real use for the skill in her life. Sure, she'd played around with it, honed it because Mihai had trained her.

"Well, Mihai told Rider I'd be joining the council, so I will."

"Does she know what you are?"

"No." For now Ryan decided not to share all that Mihai had told her. She was still processing the information about Amelia herself.

Miss Genny must know, and Ryan was willing to bet that was one of the reasons Miss Genny had wanted her to steer clear of Amelia.

"Just be careful. She clearly isn't one of us. I don't think Miss Genny's father was the vampire which means Amelia's mother isn't one."

"I know," Ryan replied. "But for some reason I can't seem to just walk away from her."

****

"Let's get some drinks." Elise pulled her to her feet and led her inside.

The doorbell rang, and Elise smiled. "Charlie. Excuse me a minute. Go ahead and help yourself to a drink or something."

Amelia glanced around the medium sized kitchen taking in the country charm. She had just made up her mind to get some water when she heard a voice.

"I can't believe you brought Hope," Elise said. "And what are we drinking?"

"Fruit tea," Charlie said.

"No Sangrias?"

"Not unless they're nonalcoholic. I did bring some wine though."

"Fantastic," she said. "Hope, your boss's niece is here. Maybe the three of us can have a glass of wine and loosen up a little."

As they came into the kitchen, Elise's arm was around Hope who looked a bit uncomfortable.

"Hey, Amelia," Hope said moving away from Elise to come to stand next to her.

"Hi. Hi, Charlie."

"Hey, girl," Charlie said with a smile.

"We can make the tea if you want to go shoot the shit with the guys," Elise said.

"I'll make it," Charlie said. "Why don't you guys go on outside."

"Fine idea," Elise said and gave Charlie a kiss on the cheek.

"I'll bring some drinks out when I'm done," Charlie volunteered.

"Make mine wine," Elise said. "Come on, ladies. Let's pick out some music." She headed out to the deck.

They selected some music, and Elise cranked it up but not as loud as Amelia had expected. Charlie brought out their drinks, and Elise got Charlie to dance with her before pulling her into a dance while Charlie and Hope danced.

To her surprise, Elise made no moves on her. She kept her hands to herself.

On a slow tune, Ryan cut in, drawing Amelia into her arms.

"Having fun yet?" Ryan asked.

"I told Elise we'd been dating for a few weeks."

"I gathered you would," she replied. "I told Ree the same. I don't want your story to fall apart."

"I'm sorry," she said with a hint of regret at putting Ryan in a situation where she had to lie to her friends.

"Forget about it," Ryan told her with a laugh. "It's nothing." She drew Amelia closer. "I like your perfume."

"Thanks," she murmured. "I like being in your arms. I feel safe."

"You are safe, Amelia."

Amelia rested her head on Ryan's shoulder and soaked up the warm strength of her as they swayed to the music. This was the only place on earth she wanted to be right now.

After dancing a few more dances, they sat down to eat. The conversation flowed around her, and laughter tingled on the air. Amelia watched them, listened to them, and marveled at how at their open conversation and warmth for each other.

She'd never really had that even in college and it made her long for this kind of camaraderie, for real friends.

After dinner they sat around the table talking some more about the people they knew and the things they had planned for the week. Even Hope was engaged in the conversation, seeming at home.

"So, you two have been sneaking around for four weeks?" Rena gave Amelia a curious look.

"Something like that," Amelia agreed giving Ryan a look finding her expression warm as she put a hand on her nape.

Her fingers were slightly calloused but soft and her hold made Amelia feel like she belonged to Ryan. She leaned toward her soaking up the open affection.

"I can't believe it," Rena exclaimed. "But you always could keep a secret."

"You know I don't kiss and tell," Ryan said sliding her hand down Amelia's back.

"Yeah, yeah," Rena grumbled. "Well, why don't we get some coffee and cake?"

"I'll make the coffee," Elise said. "You guys just sit tight."

"Ryan seemed more relaxed today," Charlie said. "I guess you have something to do with that."

Amelia glanced at Ryan and leaned into her wanting to be even closer, closer to the energy coming from her. It smelled delicious and warm.

What? What did that even mean? She quickly pushed the odd thought aside.

"I hope so," Amelia answered.

"She can be hard to read sometimes," Charlie commented. "But Ry is a good girl."

"I've noticed you guys checking each other out," Hope spoke up. "I guess you were just making out with your eyes."

Amelia grinned and kissed Ryan's jaw. There was that scent. She wanted to feast on it.

Again, she had to fight to disentangle herself from the alien thought and said, "I like that, and it is so true."

"Very true," Ryan agreed and dropped a kiss on her lips that made Amelia's stomach flutter.

It had to be too early to even be thinking about how good Ryan's lips felt on hers, how much she liked sitting close to her like this, but how soon was really too soon for love at first sight?

"Trust me, Amelia, if you have Ry, you've got a keeper," Charlie said.

"I think I will keep her," Amelia said, and she meant it.

"I know Miss Honeywell hasn't seemed that keen for you to get involved with anyone here. Is that why you've been hiding it?"

"Not at all," Amelia said not sure how to respond. "I—"

"Amelia wanted a little time to get to know me without the town intruding," Ryan cut in giving her a smile, and Amelia smiled back thanking her for coming to her rescue.

"After the other night, I just think it's time," Amelia said. It was time for her to take control of her life, and Ryan was not just the catalyst. She was also the first step.

"Good because I hate to see Ryan hiding like she's a dirty secret."

"It wasn't like that, Charlie," Ryan said defensively. "But we don't have to explain anything to you."

"You don't," Charlie agreed. "I was just saying."

"And I appreciate it," Ryan said.

"Well, I for one can't wait to see how this plays out," Hope commented giving Amelia a covert look.

Amelia had to admit, she was eager to know that herself.

Chapter Twelve

"Don't forget about those papers I sent you," Rena said as they headed for the door at dusk.

"I won't forget, Ree," Ryan assured her. "They're first up after I finish up my work tomorrow."

"I need them by one but not later than five."

"I know," Ryan said firmly. "You've told me already. Have I ever let you down?"

"No, but I know how things are at the bank."

"Relax," Ryan told her. "I have a lot on my plate, but I'm not six. I can handle it."

"Okay. Right." Ree gave her a quick hug. "Thanks."

"Not a problem."

"See you later Amelia," Ree said as she released Ryan and gave Amelia a hug.

"Thanks for inviting me," Amelia said quietly.

"Course," Ree said. "You're welcome anytime."

"Thanks."

"Night guys," Elise called. "Drive careful."

"Will do," Ryan said slipping an arm around Amelia's waist as they strolled down the walk to the driveway.

Ryan unlocked the door, and Amelia climbed in on her side while Ryan got in on hers. She clicked her seatbelt in place as Amelia did the same.

"I think that went well," Amelia said.

"The most important people will back me up when I tell Miss Genny we've been dating. And Hope will make sure to tell Kailey and it will be all around town that we've been secret lovers for a month by this time tomorrow."

Amelia laughed. "You're kidding, right?"

"That's small-town life," Ryan said and backed out.

Amelia put her hand on Ryan's thigh, and Ryan glanced at her to find Amelia looking out of the window. Ryan took Amelia's hand and held it for a moment as she drove, and her hand tingled faintly as if Amelia was drawing energy from her.

If she was, it was an unconscious act.

"I guess it's going to work out better than I'd hoped and if my mom does turn up there won't be any doubt in her mind that I'm not interested in Greg."

"Are you engaged to this guy?"

"No. I would never ask you to—No."

"Just curious because it would drive home the point if you were cheating on him," Ryan said.

"I'm not like that," Amelia said softly. "I might not be happy with the way I've allowed my life to be ordered for me, but I'm not that kind of person."

"Drastic times..."

"I shouldn't have brought you into it," Amelia said apologetically. She caressed Ryan's thigh, and Ryan's nipples hardened. "It was thoughtless."

"More like smart," Ryan said. "You show your mother you're not interested, and it works if you stand your ground."

"I plan to," she responded. "I can't keep living like this. I'm suffocating and sometimes, it physically hurts to even think of getting out of bed. I just start crying or break out in a cold sweat. I'm furious with myself for being so cowardly."

"Amelia—"

"No, Ryan. I am a coward. I feel like I should just do it. My sister did it. So, did my brother. They both have decent marriages, kids. They seem happy."

"Could you be happy with a man?"

"No."

"Then, that's the easy way out. It takes courage to stand your ground especially with your parents. They have their own expectations."

"You're lucky to have a dad who puts your happiness above his expectations."

"I am pretty lucky," Ryan murmured. "He's a great dad." Ryan heard the edge of pain in Amelia's voice and wanted to beat some sense into her mother for putting Amelia through such hell.

She deserved better than that.

They were quiet on the rest of the drive each mulling over her own thoughts. When Ryan pulled into the circular drive, she cut the engine preparing to walk Amelia inside and released her seatbelt as Amelia did the same.

They climbed out and walked up to her door.

"I had a great time," Amelia said.

"I'm glad," Ryan said.

Amelia unlocked the door and faced Ryan. "Come in?"

"Yeah. Sure. Is it okay with Miss Genny?"

"She said it was fine," Amelia said and pushed open the door and stepped inside.

Ryan followed her in, her gaze gliding down to the bunch of Amelia's ass as she moved.

"You want a drink, some iced tea or coffee? Tea?" Amelia turned, and Ryan jerked her gaze up from Amelia's backside.

"No."

"Then, let's go up to my sitting room, and I'll put on a movie."

"That sounds good," Ryan said, and followed her to the curving staircase.

"I have a small collection here," Amelia told her. "Mostly romance. Is that okay?"

"It's fine," Ryan said.

On the landing, Amelia led the way down a corridor and opened the door of a neatly appointed room.

Ryan glanced around it taking in the sofa, chair and coffee table. The room was a soft shade of sand but the soft shades of pink and purple along with the art on the walls and the stack of books on the table told her that Amelia spent a lot of time in this room. It was her.

"Artemis?" Ryan asked.

"Aunt Genny doesn't mind my interest in mythology or study of Wicca."

"You're a witch?"

"Wiccan all my life really. It's another thing my mother forbids."

"Ah." Ryan smiled. "How did that happen without your mother?"

"My grandmother told me she wasn't going to allow me to practice the evil arts that her mother and grandmother had practiced, but my grandmother began training me even before they knew it."

"Runs in the family then," Ryan murmured. "Hope is rumored to practice. Maybe you should talk to her. It could be good to have a sister witch around."

"I'll certainly bring it up."

"You should. She might be a solitary or practice with a few friends," Ryan said moving to stand in front of her.

"She does hang out with a few other women," she murmured, her eyes filling with heat that drew Ryan in.

She ran her hands up Amelia's thighs to her hips as she closed the distance between them.

"I've wanted to do this all afternoon," Ryan said in a low tone and bent her head and kissed Amelia.

Her lips parted after a moment, and Ryan's tongue swept in. She kept things easy, wanting to savor Amelia, to feel her. She ran her hands back down to tug Amelia's skirt up and push her hands beneath.

Ryan shaped her ass as her tongue dueled with Amelia's. She wanted her so bad and wondered if Amelia was using an old form of magic on her because she hadn't wanted a woman this much in a few years.

Her fires weren't out, but she had turned her focus from sex merely for the pleasure of it even before she'd admitted it to herself.

She needed more. Ryan craved a connection stronger than hormones and the beauty of a woman's face and body.

She wanted to know her deepest secrets, her joys, her fears.

"Ryan," Amelia purred and pushed at Ryan's arms.

Groaning, Ryan lifted her head. "Okay." She hadn't meant to move too fast, but there was something about Amelia that clouded her thoughts and went straight to her head.

Amelia's green gaze was dark with desire, and she gave Ryan another shove. Ryan frowned and Amelia moved past her, but not before grabbing a handful of her shirt and tugging her with her to the couch.

There she shoved Ryan, and Ryan fell onto the cushions giving Amelia a curious look. The hunger in her stare told her Amelia wasn't pushing her away.

Then, Amelia unbuttoned her blouse to reveal the black lace of her corset with interesting detailing that drew the eye right to the perfect breasts.

"Damn, baby what are you doing with that on?" Amelia was shy and sweet but that was not the bra of a shy woman.

Amelia ran a hand from the back of her neck, down the side of it and over one breast to rest on the nearly flat of her stomach.

The pale of her skin was damn enticing against the black.

"Do you think it's too—Not me?"

"It's perfectly you," Ryan murmured, wondering if her panties were equally enticing. She had to admit, she did have a thing for a woman in sexy lingerie no matter what color but red, black, and blue and even pink were her favorites.

Ryan sat forward and ran a finger down between the valley of her breasts. She cupped the firm mounds before sitting back.

"Unzip or unclip it," Ryan ordered her.

Amelia took her time releasing the tiny hooks in front baring her strawberries and cream skin. Her pert nipples were erect and pale pink berries that made Ryan's mouth water.

She licked her lips and swallowed convulsively. Amelia didn't push the top off. Instead, she reached beneath her skirt and pushed her panties down and stepped out of them before moving to straddle Ryan's lap.

Ryan gave her hips a jerk tugging her right up against the dildo she wore. Amelia gasped and Ryan smiled as she slipped her hands beneath the skirt to caress the globes of her ass.

Amelia's breath hitched, and Ryan pressed kisses along Amelia's throat and down to her chest. She slid her hands up Amelia's back and urged her back.

Amelia braced her hands on the cushion while Ryan licked a taut peak. She curled her tongue around the bud before laving the tender skin and then she drew it into her mouth and sucked.

Ryan pinched the other nipple as she took a hard draw. Then, she released the succulent flesh. She speared it with her tongue before drawing it back into her mouth for a hard pull.

At the same time, she rolled the other nipple between her fingers and pinched it. A gasp escaped Amelia and Ryan forced herself to reign part of herself in. She had to take it slow with Amelia. She couldn't just do what she wanted to her, not yet.

Ryan released the bud and licked the curve of the other breast, moving her tongue over the areola before curling around the pink pearl. She smelled like jasmine and a hint of lily.

She caught the nipple between her teeth and bit down and Amelia pushed her fingers into Ryan's hair. Ryan sucked the tender bud into her mouth, drawing a moan from Amelia.

Amelia moved on her lap, and Ryan drew her head up and claimed Amelia's mouth, the fire in her eyes spreading to Ryan.

The kiss was rough, demanding as her own arousal ramped up. Amelia's hands were on her now working the buttons of her shirt free, and Ryan let her. Amelia's hand moved inside her shirt to the black camisole Ryan wore.

She pushed her hands beneath, and Ryan sighed, the soft hands making her hotter. Amelia cupped her breasts, her touch hesitant.

Then, Amelia leaned in, her gaze liquid heat as she met Ryan's. The warmth was a caress that beckoned Ryan closer. She claimed Amelia's mouth for another kiss. This one was as hot and demanding as the last.

Amelia's hands stroked her arms, one hand pushed into her hair as Amelia strained closer, moving ever so slightly against her. Ryan's heat index climbed as the passion in her intensified.

Breaking the kiss, Amelia trailed her lips along the side of Ryan's neck.

Ryan cupped Amelia's ass, allowing her hands to stroke over her skin before striking her. Amelia gasped, but she didn't stop kissing her. Ryan hit her again, the urge to begin the dark eroticism she enjoyed pulling at her.

Not yet, she reminded herself. You don't want to scare her.

But the dark needs rode her, demanded she begin Amelia's initiation.

No.

"My belt," Ryan told her in a ragged tone as she fought the command of her darker, primal self. "Take care of it, Amelia." She kissed her again to avoid the dominant urge to bite her.

Amelia fumbled with her belt but finally got it open before moving on to the button of her pants and then the zipper. The kiss was a consuming flame, and Ryan could hardly think.

She knew what Amelia wanted and didn't see the reason to hold back. Ryan pulled the soft-skinned dick from her briefs. The fit was sublime, and the base pressed just right against her clit.

"Ryan," Amelia murmured. "Please."

"Take my dick into your tight little pussy, baby," she crooned. "Show me how much you want it."

Amelia didn't hesitate. She moved, bracing on her knees and positioned her body over the head of the cock and started to slide down.

"Slowly," Ryan told her. She like to play around with the size but thought a size eight was the perfect size for a virgin pussy.

Amelia took her in, slow and easy and Ryan watched her expression for signs of discomfort and revulsion. She wouldn't force her to do something she didn't want.

Amelia grimaced.

"Too much?" Ryan asked.

"No, just bigger than I thought," Amelia admitted shyly.

"Take your time," Ryan told her. "I want every inch of it buried in your tight cat."

Amelia shivered and her cheeks colored at the explicit word and the image it conjured.

Ryan cupped her ass and gave the tight globes a light swat. Amelia looked startled so Ryan smoothed her hand over the flesh and struck her again, keeping the tap light.

This time Amelia's green eyes flickered with pleasure. Ryan hit her a little harder, and Amelia hissed but the delectation in her eyes was all Ryan needed to know. They'd be able to move on to spankings next time.

"Ryan," Amelia begged. "It's—"

"Do you want to stop?"

"No. I—" She moved tentatively but found a groove that drew a moan of appreciation from her. Ryan let Amelia set the pace, giving her time to adjust to the toy and decide whether she liked it.

She caressed Amelia's ass and kissed the side of her neck. Amelia moved faster, hands braced on the back of the couch.

"Ryan," she moaned. "Oh, god. That feels good."

Ryan squeezed Amelia's ass as she bit her shoulder. Amelia gasped and moved even faster. Ryan drew her hands up Amelia's back, her own arousal a deluge, her pussy soaking wet and her clit hard. The stimulation was amazing, but she wasn't going to come until Amelia did.

"Oh, god," Amelia cried. "Oh!"

"Oh, shit," Ryan groaned. "Fuck." She was going to—Not yet.

Amelia's breasts bounced in her face, and Ryan lost the battle. Her need overpowering.

"Turn, Amelia," she commanded and helped Amelia turn to face the coffee table. "Hands on the table, feet firmly on the floor."

Amelia obeyed her command, and Ryan guided the soft dick back into her, watching as it slid into the wet sheath. Amelia's breathing was rough, her body relaxed.

Ryan closed her fingers around Amelia's throat and urged her back. She kissed her nape as she glided her other hand down between Amelia's legs. She found the tight bundle of nerves between them and teased lightly as she bit the side of her neck.

Amelia moaned.

Ryan licked the side of her neck forcing herself to wait. Urging Amelia forward again so she could brace her hands on the low table, Ryan drew almost all the way out before sliding back in. She went deep into the slick pocket and pulled out and drove in again.

She found her own groove, and Amelia mewled and rocked with her as Ryan took her with controlled abandon.

Ryan thrust into her, in and out, the pace just the other side of frenzied.

"Ryan. Ryan!" Amelia cried.

The need in her voice had Ryan pulling the trigger. She picked up the pace knowing Amelia was close. It was just an instinctive knowing, and she stroked into her rough and deep, and Amelia's body pulled tight as she let out a scream.

Head clouding with only one thing, Ryan sank her teeth into the throbbing pulse at Amelia's neck. Blood seeped into her mouth, and she took a draw savoring the sweetness of the warm liquid. Her eyes closed, the beat of Amelia's heart loud in her ears. Forcing herself to stop, Ryan lifted her head, trembling.

Amelia tasted exquisite. The perfect mix of sweet tart apple. She pressed her nose to Amelia's skin taking her scent in. Steadier, Ryan licked the wound knowing it would be mostly healed by morning. No one would really notice the two tiny puncture marks especially if Amelia wore her hair down.

Breathing hard, Ryan sat back on the couch pulling Amelia into her arms. Amelia turned, straddled her, and cuddled against Ryan. The fit was perfect.

Then, Ryan felt it. Just the slightest bit of a pull on her energy as Amelia nuzzled her throat. Her heart kicked and her blood rushed. Ryan tightened her arms around Amelia, waiting for her to take more. The slide of her energy from her an erotic sensation that made her wet all over again.

Sharp teeth pierced her energy field and more energy leaked from Ryan making her gasp and Amelia jerked up right. Their eyes met and the hint of surprise in wide green eyes was overshadowed by the darkness of desire.

"That was incredible," Amelia murmured in a husky tone, a drop of energy at the corner of her mouth.

Ryan stroked Amelia's back. "It was amazing." She pushed her fingers into Amelia's hair and pulled her head back for a kiss.

Amelia rested one hand on the couch as she submitted to her. Ryan tightened her fingers in Amelia's hair, and Amelia began moving against her. Amelia broke the kiss and looked down at her, heat flared in green eyes that glowed like fire.

"Oh," Amelia groaned. "Ryan." Amelia reached down to grip the cock and guided it back inside herself.

Ryan tugged on Amelia's hair pulling her head back. Amelia's gaze filled with surprise.

"I—"

"Oh, yeah, I know what you want, pretty baby," Ryan whispered. "But tell me."

"I—"

"Say it, or you can't have it."

Amelia looked at her shy but all too quickly her gaze shifted from innocent to coquette. "I want you," she said, a hint of confidence shining in her eyes and reverberating in her tone.

Ryan chuckled. "Yeah, I know you do, but I doubt that's what you're really after." No. Amelia wanted, but she wanted the rush of energy, but she couldn't yet have the talent for taking it.

"Ride my dick then, angel," she said roughly. "Give me that pussy."

Amelia rocked on her and moaned. "It feels so good."

Ryan closed her arms around her and moved quickly putting Amelia's back on the couch cushion. She pushed her arms up above her head and drove into her. The animal inside her, hungry once more thanks to the energy Amelia had taken, stirring her arousal.

"Yes," Amelia cried. "Oh, yes."

Ryan lifted one of Amelia's slim thighs onto her shoulder and drove into her slowly. Amelia shuddered and she drew back and drove in again. The strokes were even and deep.

Amelia's eyes slide closed but not before Ryan saw the delectation glowing in them. She thrust in and pulled out, drove in, keeping her pace even as she built her own arousal to fever pitch.

She released Amelia's arms, bracing her hands on the couch as she fucked her with near abandon. The need to howl tore through her as the need to feed again rode her hard, but Ryan knew once was enough for tonight.

Amelia's cries grew louder, her hands having slipped beneath Ryan's shirt. Nails pricked her skin as she thrust into Amelia, the toy hitting her clit just right with each move. Her head was spinning, and Ryan knew it wasn't just the sex.

Amelia was feeding again. The energy enticing in its scent had to be even more so for an energy vampire just awakened.

"Oh, my goddess," Amelia whispered. "Shit. Oh shit!" she let out a scream.

At the same moment, Ryan's body bowed from the orgasm that tore through her. Shit wasn't even close.

Ryan's body began to go limp, and she dipped her head to kiss Amelia's sweet lips.

"Damn, that's good pussy," Ryan murmured.

Amelia laughed shyly holding her stare, her own drowsy and sated.

Suddenly the energy currents in the room changed and Ryan's wolf scented the intruder. She throttled a growl.

"Oh, my god."

The whispered words were filled with shock that reverberated through the room tearing Amelia away from Ryan. Her eyes widened at the sight of her sister staring at them in horror.

"What the hell are you doing, Amelia!" Grace screamed. "I—You need to get up and you—" She pointed at Ryan. "need to leave, now before I call the police and tell them you were raping her."

"You will do no such thing," Amelia snapped as Ryan slowly pulled out of her.

The other woman's gaze went to their bodies, and she reddened. "Amelia, what are you doing? Greg has a perfectly good dick, and you let this-this lesbo use that thing on you."

Ryan laughed at the embarrassment on the other woman's face as she rose.

"Grace," Amelia said as Ryan got to her feet and tucked the toy in. "It's my business who I let use what on me."

"What are you wearing? If Mother could see you now dressed like a cheap slut, she'd be horrified."

"*I* am horrified," Amelia growled. "You barged into my space without so much as a knock and—"

"I heard you scream," Grace interjected. "Twice. I thought—"

"I was having the best orgasm of my life," Amelia muttered. "So, get out, Grace. You're interrupting a private moment. She was just about to butt fuck me."

"Filthy—Get dressed," Grace commanded coldly. "I want to see you downstairs in ten minutes." She turned and stormed out.

"Whoa, that was intense," Ryan drawled. "I'll clean up and get out of here, so you two can talk."

"You don't have to."

"I gather she's never seen you with a girlfriend."

"No." Amelia tucked strands of hair behind her ear. "She's probably calling our mother to report back to her."

"Hmm. I'd never rat my sister out unless she was doing something that could change the course of her life."

"She doesn't care about my happiness," Amelia said reaching out to touch Ryan. "I'll show you where the bathroom is, but mind if I go first? I'm going to go talk to her, but I'm not ready for you to leave. I still want to watch a movie."

"Sure, but butt fucked?"

Amelia turned pink and Ryan laughed.

"Oh, don't worry, pretty baby," Ryan said. "That's a fantasy I don't mind making happen sometime."

Amelia laughed nervously. "Ryan. You're bad."

"And you like how it feels, don't you?" she asked and kissed Amelia. "Go ahead. Get cleaned up." Ryan's first instinct was just to leave, but Amelia seemed to need her to stay, so she straightened her clothes and waited for Amelia to clean up.

When Amelia returned, she had changed into a pair of lounge pants and t-shirt. Her hair cascaded over her shoulders, and she'd washed the make-up from her face revealing the pretty beneath.

Ryan got to her feet. "You're beautiful without the make-up," she said knowing that could be the wrong thing to say.

Amelia gave her a shy smile. "Thanks." Amelia closed the distance between them and kissed her. "You were even more amazing the second time."

"So were you, pretty baby," Ryan murmured. "Now, show me where to clean up before we get into round three and Grace ends up having a heart attack instead of a conniption fit."

Amelia laughed wickedly and showed her the bathroom before leaving her alone, and Ryan cleaned up before planting her butt back on the couch to wait though she wanted to be hold Amelia's hand.

However, if Amelia couldn't stand up to her family, this wasn't going any further.

Chapter Thirteen

Amelia headed for the kitchen with the intent of making popcorn, and she heard voices from the breakfast room and veered off. Her sister was there with her husband.

"Get in here, Amelia," Grace ordered.

"I'm not your child, Grace," Amelia told her evenly. "I'm a grown woman who's entit—"

"Who's virtually engaged," Grace snapped. "What were you thinking?" Grace got to her feet, hands pressing to her hips as she glared at her. "Do you have any idea what a disgrace your depravity is?"

"Depravity?" she asked softly.

"Exactly. You get your act together. In fact, I came down here to take you home. We're leaving in the morning."

"I'm not going anywhere," Amelia replied quietly. "I am home, and Ryan is my girlfriend. It's my prerogative to have sex with her whenever I want."

"Do you hear yourself?" Grace growled.

"And for a change I'm going to listen to me," she said coldly.

"You can't have sex with another woman. It's not real sex. She was wearing a strap-on for God's sake!"

"It was damn good sex, and I think I'm going to have some more before the night is over," Amelia retorted.

"Amelia if I tell Mother what I just saw, you'll lose your inheritance. Does that dyke know that?"

"What she knows isn't your concern, Grace, but you should be happy I'm not coming back. Mother will start pinching off my inheritance, and I'm sure she'll share with you since you are her favorite."

"A—"

"I'm not moving back there. I'm going to stay right here where I'm happy, and where I'm free. You can tell Mother that or better yet take out your phone, and I'll say it again and you can play it back to her when she asks why you didn't manage to bully me into coming back."

"You can't do this," Grace snapped.

"I can and I will," Amelia said and exited the room. She went into the kitchen and retrieved a tray from the pantry.

"Amelia, you're making a big mistake," Grace told her.

"I've allowed myself to be imprisoned. No more. I'm out on bail, and I'm making a run for the border." She shrugged and happiness coursed through her at the new possibilities for life here.

Amelia retrieved popcorn from a cupboard and put the bag into the microwave."

"Fine. Be a pauper if that's what you want, but you'll find it a very pathetic existence."

"At least it'll be my choice," she said softly. At least she wouldn't wake up in a cold sweat from the anxiety her life had devolved to.

"Whatever you say." Grace made a quick retreat, and Amelia exhaled a long slow breath.

With shaking hands, she got two bottles of tea from the fridge and two bottles of water. Then, Amelia grabbed a chocolate bar and put the items on a tray.

When the popcorn stopped, she pulled it from the microwave and poured it into a bag.

She was doing the right thing. There was no question. She owed it to herself to take control of her own life, to be happy or miserable on her own terms.

A smile curved her lips, and Amelia grabbed some napkins and took the tray upstairs.

"Ryan," she called once she'd made it back up to her wing. "Ryan."

The door opened, and Ryan took the tray from her.

"You should have come got me. I'd have carried this up," she said.

"Thanks, but I managed just fine. I didn't need a big strong butch."

"Oh, no?" Ryan teased setting the tray down.

"No." She smiled. "But I wouldn't mind having one."

Amelia walked over to Ryan who caught her in a hug, and Amelia laughed as Ryan swung her around before collapsing onto the couch.

"There are plenty of things a big strong butch is good for," Ryan murmured.

"Like what?" Amelia asked in a low tone. "I've never had one around."

"Oh, well. I could spend all night educating you, but I think we'll take our time and let you learn as you go," Ryan replied, her hand gliding up Amelia's back.

"I see you selected a movie," Amelia murmured and kissed Ryan. She straddled her, giving herself over to the kiss.

She moaned as Ryan's tongue slowly made love to her. Her body heated and her pussy moistened as her nipples hardened.

"Is this one of those things?" Amelia asked breathlessly.

"Just one of many," Ryan agreed, kissing her again. "We're good for movie nights too."

"One of my favorites," Amelia murmured. "I can't wait, but I must confess. I'm a purist in so many ways when it comes to Pride and Prejudice, but I kind of like this one. I must admit though that Bingley is awful." Amelia laughed.

"I've never seen it, so I'm looking forward to not liking it."

Amelia grinned. "Well, sit back and enjoy."

****

Genny arrived home to quiet and suspicion drifted through her. The sisters weren't fighting?

They must be in their respective spaces. It meant they'd settled things or had for the night. She was curious how Amelia was weathering her mother's demands.

If Amelia was set on staying, then, she was probably in need of a bit of moral support. She'd need to know it was okay for her to do what was right for herself.

Genny had thought Amelia was a fitting heir and was looking forward to bringing her into the coven.

Amelia reminded Genny of her mother in a few ways. Genny's mother had been soft-spoken and sweet. However, she'd burned hot beneath the façade of an innocent.

Genny didn't think that last applied to Amelia, but she did think this would be the perfect place and time for Amelia to come fully into herself as she had and as her mother before her had done.

Her mother had called the inn the property of an independent woman, and Genny, like her mother, had embraced that since her husband's death and even before.

Genny hoped Amelia would as well.

Genny made her way to Amelia's wing. A light was on in the sitting room, and she opened the door and peeked inside finding Amelia curled up in Ryan's arms. Her hand rested on Ryan's stomach.

She slipped into the room and picked up the throw from a nearby chair and spread it over them with a smile. So, Amelia's fight began. She'd stand by her no matter what Felicia tried to pull.

Her phone rang as she reentered her bedroom, and Genny went to take it from her purse, a smile playing on her lips.

"Hello, Felicia," she said quietly.

"Do you know what's going on in your home?" she demanded.

"To what are you referring, Felicia?" she asked with a frown.

"Grace told me she caught Amelia in the act of depravity with another woman."

Genny had to laugh at that. "Really? Amelia was having sex with her girlfriend? I guess that really freaked Grace out since she's never seen two people having sex before."

"Genny," Felicia growled. "How could you allow that woman to force herself on Amelia?"

"Amelia was the one who told me she and Ryan were dating."

"Ryan? Who's Ryan?"

"Ryan is the woman's name," Genny said patiently as she entered her bedroom. "Amelia is an adult—"

"Who is a hair from losing her inheritance. Either she comes home tomorrow or that's it."

"I'll inform her of that if I speak to her before you do," Genny said. "But I urge you to reconsider. Let Amelia stay here for the rest of the year and the next and maybe get this out of her system."

"Get this out of her s—She's an embarrassment," Felicia muttered. "I bet she's parading around town with that—I'm coming down there with Greg. Once she sees him, she'll realize how serious I am."

"Felicia don't be so rash," she said on a sigh. "You'll risk isolating your daughter. I'm sure that's the last thing you want to do."

"I'll handle this," Felicia told her. "You just make sure you get a room at the house ready for me and Greg."

"You and Greg can stay at the inn," Genny replied evenly. "I won't h—"

"It's my house too," Felicia cut in. "It's our father's property which comes to me on your death. So, it's mine too. I'll expect two rooms waiting for us."

"Fine. Whatever you want, Felicia. When can I expect you?"

"Tomorrow afternoon."

"I'll be at the inn, but you just come to the house and my houseman will show you two to your rooms."

"Then, we'll come to the inn."

"That's not the best idea," Genny said. "But—"

"I know what's best for my own daughter," she cut in, coldly. "The sooner Amelia realizes what's at stake the sooner she'll do what's right."

"I guess you're right."

"We'll be gone by tomorrow night. You'll get the house back to yourself sooner rather than later."

"I'll see you tomorrow then." Genny ended the call and sighed. She may as well try to sleep because tomorrow was going to be a very trying day.

Chapter Fourteen

Amelia woke the next morning alone stretched out on the couch, the TV off. A smile tipped her lips, and she stretched feeling as if sunshine lit her soul from the inside out.

She'd never felt this happy before or as if the day was full of promise that could only make her life worth looking forward to with each minute that passed. Yet this morning she did, and it was all because of Ryan.

She sat up and made her way to her bedroom hunger pricking at her only her stomach wasn't growling. This hunger was different. Amelia frowned unable to grasp the need that curled around her.

She pushed it aside deciding to grab some toast and tea before work as she came to a stop at her dresser where she picked up her phone. The light crisp scent of Ryan drifted over her, and her nipples hardened as the memory of last night played through her mind.

Amelia smiled, hand caressing her stomach as she checked the time and found a message. She opened it finding one from her mother and one from Ryan.

She read the one from Ryan, her stomach fluttering with excitement.

I'll see you later. Had to go.

Amelia smiled again and put her phone down. She took a quick shower taking care to moisturize before slipping into panties and bra. A smile pushed at her lips as she recalled the lingerie she'd worn yesterday.

Buying those pieces had been crazy, but she was glad she'd taken the risk now.

Amelia finished dressing in a pair of casual pants that were part of a suit. The blouse was dainty and feminine and would go on over her camisole. Then, she rummaged through her meager jewelry box for a necklace and earrings. Only the pieces she'd loved had made the trip with her.

The expensive jewelry her mother had bought for certain events had been to make a statement that Amelia could care less about. Here, the living was so much easier. However, she would have to pick up a few things to round out her wardrobe.

Amelia stepped into flats and moved to the dresser to do her hair. As she combed the fine locks, she noticed the faint edges of gold on her skin just above the edge of her cami that seemed to form a necklace. She moved in closer to the mirror, fingers going to the charm that became ever more visible.

She blinked as the warm metal took stronger form. It was a crest with roses and ivy vines crawling around the letters, RB. The crest rose when she lifted it, but Amelia released it, startled.

Her breathing picked up as she stared at the metal just lying on her chest. She touched it again, and this time, she pulled it free and looked at it. It could be an amulet of sorts, but it was small enough to be worn as a charm.

She put it on the dresser and noise from outside drew her to the window. Amelia reached for the curtain and started to draw it back, but the sun kissed her skin burning her. She drew back with a gasp and looked at her hand finding a burn across the back of her hand that extended down to her wrists.

The pain that licked a path across her flesh made her wince, and she stepped back from the window. Amelia glanced to the dresser where the charm was and went to pick it up.

Nothing had happened to her when she had it on, so laid it on the burn and her skin immediately began to cool. Then, the amulet vanished becoming part of her skin.

She could still see it; it looked like nothing more than a tattoo. She caressed her hand, deciding to leave it where it was for now.

She'd ask her aunt if this was some type of magical protection against—A sun allergy?

She didn't recall ever being allergic to the sun, she mused with a frown.

Her aunt would know, but her mother might—Why had her mother used magic? Her grandmother despised it and hushed up any talk about the family history of witchcraft.

But she had found two books in the sitting room of her great-grandmother's bedroom after her great-grandmother had died. Amelia had been just twelve and had found more solace in being alone in that room with her pain than sipping tea and listening to her mother and grandmother give orders to the servants.

They hadn't kept many of her great-grandmother's things. Just some jewelry and a few items of clothing, but the rest had been given away and the house sold as if they'd been trying to wipe away their heritage.

Amelia paced her bedroom as fragments of stories came back to her. She'd been no more than five when her great-grandmother had begun telling her those stories.

"I wish I could do magic," Amelia had said.

"Oh, my dear, but you can," she murmured and smiled. "You have magic inside of you that's rooted deep in the heart of you. Don't let anybody tell you different."

She didn't have the books with her, and she'd never read the books she'd taken. However, she had used that old cookbook that her grandmother had willed to her along with a few cooking utensils.

She had to get that. Amelia was certain she'd find proof of her family's magical history in those old recipes.

Amelia exhaled softly and stared at her reflection. She had to ask about the crest, she mused, her gaze going to the tiny punctures on the side of her neck. She moved in a little closer to the mirror. Amelia frowned at the fading marks as she caressed them wondering how she'd gotten them.

Had to have been in the park yesterday. They didn't hurt and they didn't appear to be swollen. Had to be a bush or something. She'd keep an eye on it to see if she developed any swelling, redness or anything that could indicate trouble, she decided and put her hair up using a couple of pretty combs.

Then, Amelia slipped into her blouse, buttoned it, and grabbed her jacket and pulled it on. Next, she picked up her purse, phone and keys and headed downstairs with a spring in her step.

She was looking forward to seeing Ryan later. Amelia hoped Ryan planned to take her out tonight because she really wanted to spend the evening with her now that she didn't have to hide anymore.

In the breakfast room, there was silence, but her aunt was there alone with her tablet.

"Good morning, Auntie," she said brightly.

"Good morning, Amelia," her aunt said giving her a smile. "You're glowing. I guess you had a good time with Ryan last night."

Amelia giggled feeling like a schoolgirl. "I did."

"Have you talked to your mother this morning?"

"No. Why?" she asked as she hung her purse on her chair and put her phone on the table before going to the sideboard to put toast and eggs on a plate.

"She called last night."

Amelia moved to the table and sat down, pouring herself a cup of tea. She added sugar and lemon and took a sip. "I imagine that Grace told her what she saw," Amelia said with a shrug. "But I don't care."

"No?" Her aunt lifted her brows.

"It's time I started living my life not the one she wants."

"That's a good start."

"I have to go close up my apartment and pack my things, and give notice, but this is my home now."

"You're serious?"

"Yes, and Mother is going to find that out the hard way. I know it's early to be asking for time off, but—"

"You can take three or four days to go take care of things later in the week."

"Great." She beamed and picked up her phone to call Ryan.

"Amelia?"

"Yes?" She paused in her dialing to look at her aunt, the tone of her voice holding concern.

"What happened to your neck?" She rubbed the side of her own indicating the spot on Amelia's.

"I guess something bit me," she said and rubbed her skin. This time her touch brought a flash of memory. Ryan had bitten her when they'd been having sex, but that couldn't be what caused those two tiny marks.

"Did Ryan bite you?"

"Uh—It didn't cause that though." She gave a little laugh.

"But she did bite you?"

"It wasn't—Yes." Unease at talking about her sex life slithered through her. She set her phone down. "Aunt Genny, I wanted to ask you something now that you mention that."

"What is it?"

Amelia held out her hand. "I've never seen this before, but I—Do you know anything about it?"

Her aunt stared. "It's your father's family crest," she answered carefully. "It was put on you when you were a child by a witch doctor."

"Why?" she asked carefully.

"Because of your sun allergy. It was slowly killing you. Nothing any doctor did ever helped, but the witch doctor used that crest. It's magical protection against the sun. If you take it off, you'll burn."

"Why have I never seen it?" she asked with a frown.

"Maybe the medicine needs to be renewed," her aunt answered. "I'll find out."

Amelia studied her. "Who—Mom's not into witch magic."

"Your father," she said. "He was desperate. You were in such bad shape, practically suffocating to death and your skin was burning. It was a last resort and it worked."

"Okay, how can I find out if it's wearing off? I got a sun burn before I came here, and I had the amulet on."

"I'll hire someone to find him," she said.

Amelia nodded. "Thanks."

"Your mother is coming here today." Her aunt changed the subject, and Amelia didn't know whether to be relieved or annoyed.

Amelia rolled her eyes. "I'm sure she's bringing Greg."

"She mentioned that. They'll be staying here."

"If she thinks that's going to change anything, she's wrong," Amelia said picking up her phone and beginning to dial Ryan again. "I don't want to make the drive on my own, so I'm going to see if I can get Ryan to go with me."

"You really like her."

Amelia smiled. "Yes. I do. Hi, Ryan. Hold on a minute. Excuse me, Auntie."

Her aunt gave her a nod.

"Good morning, sweetie," Ryan murmured in her ear. "I hope you aren't sore from sleeping on that couch."

"I'm fine," she said, warmth rippling through her. "I was about to say the same thing about you."

"Not by much," she answered. "I hope Miss Genny isn't too upset about that."

"About you staying the night?" she asked, looking at her aunt whose head was down bent.

"Exactly. I guess I was a little tired. Tell her it won't happen again."

"Then, I'll have to stay at your place," Amelia said softly, unable to believe she was saying that.

Ryan chuckled in her ear. "Don't think it can't be arranged, Red."

She grinned, something inside her taking wing. "I hope so. I also hope you can take off a few days later this week."

"What am I going to be doing?"

"Helping me get my apartment closed up and moving some things back here."

"I can do that," Ryan told her. "We can rent a moving truck if you need to move furniture or anything, and I'll get Charlie or Ree to drive my truck back."

"That is very sweet, but I don't have much. It's just a few things that should fit in the back of your truck. Auntie is Friday okay?"

"Fine."

"Does that work for you Ryan? I'll only need a few hours to get everything taken care of."

"Works fine."

"Thanks. You have no idea how grateful I am."

"You can show me because I expect to be paid," she replied in a low tone that made Amelia wet.

She glanced at her aunt. "I think we'll be able to work something out."

"I'm counting on you to be resourceful," Ryan purred.

"We'll talk about this later," she said.

"Can I see you for lunch?"

"What time were you thinking?"

"One."

"Just come by the inn. I'll arrange for us to have lunch in the dining room or find out if Aunt Genny will let me have one of the private rooms."

"Whatever you want to do," Ryan murmured.

"Just call me when you get there."

"I'll see you later, baby."

"Bye." She grinned, happiness bubbles in her blood.

"I guess you and Ryan had a nice night."

"Oh, Auntie, Ryan is fantastic."

Genny laughed. "That good."

"In bed and out." She clamped a hand over her mouth and her aunt reached across the table and put a hand on hers.

"You can tell me anything, Amelia. I'm not going to judge you," she said. "And if you want to have some girl talk, then, that's fine too."

Amelia sighed. "I'm just not used to—Mom never—"

"I'm not your mother," Genny said patting her hand. "I'm here for you as a friend, an aunt, whatever you need."

"Thank you, Aunt Genny," she said softly. "Thanks for hiring me. If you'd have said no, I'd have to try and find a job here."

Her aunt smiled. "I'm glad you'll be here to take care of things so I can travel a little bit."

"It'll be my pleasure."

"Now that's settled." Her aunt's expression became serious. "Now, how long have you and Ryan really been dating?"

"Four weeks. Maybe five, but it just happened." The timing might not be the same but that was the truth. Things had just happened.

Their eyes had met across the dining room, and Amelia had felt drawn to her as if pulled by a magnet. And she'd gone to Ryan's table unable to change course.

"Good morning, Aunt Genny, Amelia." Grace came into the room and poured herself some coffee from the sideboard. "Mother is coming down today, and I suggest you pull yourself together."

"I don't need to pull myself together, Grace," Amelia murmured. "It's time I did something I wanted and that something is Ryan."

"You're too old to be confused, Amelia," Grace muttered. "And stop being so selfish. Your decisions impact the family."

"Then, the family needs to learn to accept me for who I am or just pretend I don't exist," she said. "Because I will continue to date Ryan."

"After Mother talks to you, I'm sure you'll see reason."

"Reason or threats?" she demanded. "I'm tired of living that way. That money doesn't mean enough to me anymore." She got to her feet. "I'll see you at work, Auntie." Amelia picked up her phone and purse and breezed out of the room and almost ran into Victor, Grace's husband. "Excuse me."

"Morning Amelia," he said.

"Morning."

"For the record, Greg isn't worth it," he said quietly and gave her a little smile. "Sounds like this Ryan is good for you."

She frowned.

"I'd grab my chance at happiness rather than allowing it to slip away," he said evenly. "You deserve it."

She nodded slowly and walked away. He probably knew that her sister would get part of her inheritance and they could use the money. Her sister lived above their means with her expensive tastes.

Amelia was glad she didn't. The job didn't appear to be more than 45-50,000 a year, but that would be enough.

****

"Ryan." Her boss's voice drew her head up. He stood in the doorway wearing a cool mask.

"Yes, Mr. Evers?" she asked.

"You put in for a few days off after resigning?"

"I—"

"Why don't you go ahead and make tomorrow your last day," he said coolly. "I hired someone this morning, so I can put them to work. You can orientate them today and tomorrow."

"That sounds fine," she replied surprised but glad for the reprieve. "I'll clear my desk today, so they can have a space to get set up."

"Fine," he said. "I hope going to work for Rena will be worth throwing away a good job."

"I'm sure I'll make the best of it," she answered.

He gave her a nod. "Forward all paperwork to your supervisor."

"Will do." That was another reason she was leaving this job.

She had been passed over for a promotion not once but twice, and Ryan believed it was merely because she was a woman. It was time she put this place in her rear view and move onto someplace that appreciated her.

"I'll send him in. His name is Barton Cranston. He's my nephew. He just moved here from Oklahoma."

She nodded. Ryan had heard the name tossed around a few times before she decided to quit. She'd thought Barton was going to take her place, and she'd be put out front as a teller.

"Sure," she said. Ryan sighed and sat back in her chair. She wondered if the owner of the bank was aware that Evers was giving jobs away to his family and children of his friends.

Well, once he realized his bank was going down the tubes, he'd check it out and it could be too late.

She got back to work expecting to be interrupted any second. When she looked up again, it was nearly one. Ryan gathered the files she'd finished and sent them to her supervisor and logged out of her computer.

She went in search of a box and returned to her office to pack up her few personal things. Ryan took them to her truck and climbed in.

The drive to the inn was quick, and she messaged Amelia to let her know she was there before heading inside. Amelia came to meet her in the foyer of the old building.

"Hi," Amelia said with a smile.

Ryan turned. "Hey, beautiful," she answered and pulled Amelia into a hug when she came to a stop in front of her. She dropped a kiss on Amelia's lips and then groaned. "Sorry about that."

"No worries," Amelia said with a smile. "Isn't that what girlfriends do?"

Ryan smiled. "You're working that."

"Why not?" Amelia asked sliding her hands up Ryan's arms. "I'm enjoying having a girlfriend."

"In that case..."

Amelia went on tiptoe and kissed her. Ryan pushed a hand into Amelia's hair, her lips parting beneath the gentle assault.

A low whistle broke out behind them followed by teasing laughter, and Amelia broke the kiss and turned to find one of the inn's housekeepers.

"Here I thought you were an ice queen," she said. "Ryan you and Ree always get all the best girls."

Amelia gave the woman a startled look, but she laughed as she headed out the door. Then, Amelia looked up into her eyes, and Ryan smiled at the sparkle she saw there.

"I arranged for us to have a private room but if you'd prefer, we can dine in the dining room."

"It's up to you," Ryan replied.

"I want to be alone with you," Amelia said. "I like that better. No sharing."

Ryan laughed, her hand slipping down Amelia's back to her ass. "Whatever you want."

"Well, I want to see you tonight," Amelia said shyly.

"No way I'd turn down an opportunity to spend the evening with you."

"Great," Amelia said breathlessly, and Ryan saw the excitement in her green eyes.

Damn the woman was beautiful with a sweet smile that made Ryan want to take all kinds of chances with her.

"Come on. I'm starving. I didn't actually get to have breakfast this morning."

Ryan allowed Amelia to lead her from the foyer to the private dining room. It was a small room that could accommodate maybe ten people. A table was set for two with a small fruit display as the centerpiece.

The lights were low, and candles provided a soft romantic glow.

She glanced at Amelia to find her watching her, uncertainty on her face. "This is nice," Ryan said.

"Well, have a seat, and I'll be right back with our meal," she responded.

Ryan went into the room, and Amelia returned ten minutes later pushing a cart with covered dishes and a carafe of what looked like tea.

"I wasn't sure if you'd like wine, but I brought tea."

"That's fine," Ryan said getting to her feet. "I'm still on the clock. I'm supposed to be training this guy, so I'd rather not have any alcohol in my system. I hold my liquor just fine, but I don't want this guy to have any reason to complain or lie."

"Training?" Amelia looked up at her, with eyes that seemed to caress her, and Ryan felt the touch on her heart.

"He's my replacement. The boss wants me to orientate him today and tomorrow," Ryan said recovering quickly from the unexpected emotion. "Then, I'm done. I'll tell Miss Genny I'll be able to start next week."

"It'll be great having you so close," Amelia said putting a hand on her arm.

"As close as I'll be, I'll still have to put in some hours with Ree," she said. "I took the job before your aunt asked me to take over the position here."

"Why did she? I thought Leah was doing okay."

"Talk to your aunt about it," Ryan told her.

Amelia nodded. "Well, sit down and I'll serve," she said.

Ryan took a seat at the table and Amelia immediately reached onto the tray and passed her a packet. While Ryan used the contents it to clean her hands, Amelia put the plates on the table along with their tea. Then, she sat down across from Ryan.

Ryan took in the light meal of shrimp scampi with linguine with buttered rolls.

Ryan picked up her napkin roll and unrolled it eagerly. "Did you make this?"

"Yes," she said with a shy smile. "I cook."

"I bet you do," Ryan murmured.

Amelia struck her as the marrying kind. This would be a wife who made meals important and quality time even more important. She'd be a nurturing mother and devoted wife.

Ryan was looking for someone who enjoyed the traditional role, but she hadn't met anyone like that yet. Well, until maybe now.

She dug into the meal and took a small taste. The flavors were almost perfect. Not enough garlic, but she suspected that would always be the case.

"Perfect," Ryan said after swallowing. "Thanks."

Amelia started eating then. "I know it's crazy, but the truth is I'd rather be a housewife than a working woman, but given my circumstances, I'd work. I wouldn't want my wife pulling all the load on her own."

"Why not?" Ryan asked curiously.

"She'd be stressed and eventually become unhappy at the burden placed on her. I'm a capable woman. But she'd have to help out around the house. You know, make sure the trash was taken out, the lawn was mowed, and things got fixed. She'd have to help out with the dishes on the weekends."

"What about kids?" Ryan asked swirling pasta around her fork.

"I want at least two, but I'd go for three if I had boys the first time. I want at least one girl."

Ryan laughed. "What if you have three boys."

"Then, I'd press for a fourth try."

Ryan chuckled. "I can see that about you. I think you'd be a good mother."

"You don't want kids?"

"No. I do," Ryan said. "The sex isn't important. They'd both be equally wanted."

"I wouldn't not want my sons," Amelia said defensively. "I just want a girl."

"I understand, Amelia," Ryan assured her. "I just want healthy kids."

"Me too, but I want a girl to do girl things with. Maybe I can have with my daughter what I always wanted with my mother."

Ryan nodded. "It's possible," she said reaching across the table to caress Amelia's hand where it rested on the table. "Baby, you can't get back something you never had. All you can do is create a life you want."

"I know. I won't be trying to make my daughter me and me my mother."

"You're a lovely woman, Amelia. I sense you have so much kindness and love to give. I also get the feeling you're pretty smart too."

"What are you trying to say?"

"That you'd make a terrific wife and mother, and I'd be glad to have a woman like you in my life."

She nodded. "But I'm too needy?"

"Where in what I just said hinted that I thought you were needy? I think you're a strong woman to finally break free from a situation that's crushing you."

Amelia removed her hand and picked up her glass of tea. "My life—It's my fault."

"Yeah. It is," Ryan agreed. "But the fact you're doing something about it, makes you brave and strong. You're willing to accept the loss of comforts and maybe your family just to carve out your own path. I'm proud of you."

She took a sip of tea. "I'm going to miss the financial advantages, but I'm tired of being alone and unhappy. I admit I am needy but not desperate."

Ryan shook her head. "I didn't mean to imply that you were. In fact, I feel pretty lucky that you chose me."

Amelia blinked. "You do?"

"Yeah. You could have made a move on someone else leaving me to kick my own ass for not making a move sooner."

Amelia gave her a soft smile. "You were going to ask me out?"

"When I saw you at the dance, I knew it was my chance."

"Why then?"

"Your aunt told me to back off even though I'd planned to ask you out when I saw you at the Farmer's Market."

"She was just trying to protect me," Amelia murmured.

"She cares about you, and so do I."

Emotions flitted across Amelia's face, fear, hope. Then, she ducked her head, and Ryan continued eating waiting for Amelia's response.

"I'd—I want to spend more time with you too," she said softly.

Ryan was tempted to say more but decided there was plenty of time.

Chapter Fifteen

Amelia cleared their dishes away and put a dish of cookies on the table. She had thought of something more decadent but decided that should be for dinner rather than lunch.

Ryan tried one of the cookies and nodded. "Good."

"Chocolate chip walnut," Amelia said. "I made sugar and snickerdoodle and peanut butter too."

"Peanut butter is my favorite," Ryan said reaching for one. She tried it out. "Love these too."

Amelia grinned. A woman who loved to eat her cooking as much as she loved cooking. That would be a dream come true.

"I made some for you to take with you."

"I'll certainly take them," Ryan assured her as she finished off her cookie.

Amelia helped herself to a cookie. "I'll probably be having dinner with my mother tonight, but I—Would you like to come by for dessert?"

Ryan looked at her watch. "I can swing that."

"Come to the house, and we'll have it on the patio." Amelia smiled.

"With all that moonlight," Ryan said in a teasing tone. "I think you might just have something else on your mind Miss Rose-Brier."

Amelia laughed shyly. "Ryan," she chastised.

Ryan grinned and got to her feet. "I think you like making out with me in the dark."

Amelia smiled, her cheeks coloring.

"That's okay," Ryan said in a low tone. "I love the way you want me."

Amelia looked away as she stood too, but Ryan could see the color deepen in her cheeks. "Ryan, you really are funny."

"But honest." Ryan took Amelia in her arms. "Thanks for lunch beautiful. I really enjoyed it."

"I enjoyed making it for you."

Their gazes held for a long moment, and Ryan felt the warmth to her toes. She bent her head resting her forehead against Amelia's for a moment before kissing her.

Amelia moaned and curved a hand around Ryan's nape, and Ryan leaned closer savoring the feel of the other woman. It had been such a long time since she thought she could spend the day listening to a woman, wanting to hear her voice, to know what she was thinking.

And she'd woken with Amelia on her mind and fallen asleep thinking about her rather than the movie they'd been watching.

Damn was she starting to fall for this shy woman?

She certainly loved her kisses.

Amelia strained closer, and Ryan slipped an arm around her waist.

"Doesn't seem like I can get close enough to you," Amelia murmured, her voice a whisper.

"I feel the same way," Ryan said and kissed her again, the heat coming over her as the intensity of the kiss increased.

"Amelia Amaia Rose-Brier!"

The shocked gasp was like cold-water all-over Amelia. Ryan felt her shiver and then go taut.

She caressed her back holding her close even as they broke the kiss.

"Mother," Amelia said timidly.

The willowy woman with dark blonde hair strode towards them with a man on her heels. He was a half an inch taller than Ryan and wore a cold scowl that made her want to punch him.

"Amelia," he said angrily as he reached them and grabbed her arm and tugged her away from Ryan. He turned his gaze on Ryan. "We should file charges for assault."

"The only person getting assaulted is you if you don't let her go," Ryan told him as Amelia tried to pull out of his grip, but he tightened it.

"Let go," Amelia said insistently.

"Stop it, Amelia," he hissed. "You've embarrassed me enough."

"It's time you left," the woman said. "Amelia your disgraceful behavior is becoming tiresome."

"Greg, get your hands off me," Amelia snapped.

Ryan moved around the woman going behind Greg. She grabbed his free arm and twisted it behind his back. When he released Amelia, Ryan let him go and he turned.

Greg swung on her, and she blocked easily and drove a punch into his stomach causing him to double over. Ryan shoved him and he stumbled back a few steps.

"Don't put your hands on her again," Ryan growled. "And when a lady says let her go, it means just that or are you one of those guys that has a problem understanding the concept of no means no?"

"Who the hell are you?" Greg demanded glaring at Ryan.

"She is my girlfriend," Amelia said, a hint of defiance in her tone as she moved to stand next to Ryan. "Ryan, this is Greg and my mother Felicia Allen. Mother, Greg, this is Ryan Baptist." She smiled up at Ryan.

Ryan pulled her closer and the warmth in Amelia's eyes made her heart skip a beat. "Aren't you the daring one." She kissed the tip of her nose.

"Amelia," Felicia snapped. "Stop this. I will disinherit you if you don't come home with me tonight."

"I'm not going," Amelia said.

"I want you to clear your things out of the apartment by next week this time."

"I will," she said.

"You're making a mistake," Felicia told her. "Once I make the lawyers aware that you've forfeited your inheritance there's no going back."

"I know," she said. "But I'd rather be happy than imprisoned. I want a woman who loves me for me not because of my family's name or their connections."

"You think she loves you?" Greg demanded. "She thinks your aunt can further her crappy life in this crappy little town."

Ryan rolled her eyes. Everyone thought she'd come back home mostly tail dragging and whipped by the city. Yeah, she'd been beaten but by no means broken.

"She won't be able to take care of you," Felicia told Amelia.

"I can take care of myself," Amelia told her. "I have a job just like I have for years, Mother."

"Genny's generosity will run dry once she realizes you aren't going anywhere, and you can't run the inn," Felicia muttered. "You don't have the brains for it."

"Then, I'll get a job someplace else," she answered quietly. "I'm not afraid of working."

"You only got that job at the library because of me," Felicia told her. "No one wanted to hire you, but I paid them too."

Amelia let out a gasp, and Ryan saw the hurt on her face. If Felicia hadn't been a woman and Amelia's mother, she'd have hit her.

"How did such a sweet woman come from such a bitch?" Ryan asked softly, her tone hard.

"This bitch will make your life hell if you don't walk away now," Felicia growled.

"Bring it on, baby," Ryan told her.

"Amelia—"

"I don't have anything to say to you, Mother," she cut her off quietly. "Ryan, I'll see you tonight?"

"Yeah, sweetie."

Amelia hurried from the room tears in her eyes, and Ryan wanted to rip the woman's head off. Then, drain the man with her before throwing their lifeless bodies into a landfill.

"Your daughter is a terrific woman, but I guess you measure that by the amount of shit she's willing to take. I'm not going to let you hurt her."

"Worry about yourself," Felicia retorted.

"I can take whatever you want to dish out, lady," Ryan responded icily. "I know how to play hardball when it's necessary."

"Your little life in this town won't be worth my trouble," Felicia told her raking her with her gaze and Ryan gave her a cold smile.

"I'm glad you don't think so," Ryan murmured. She headed for the door going in search of Amelia.

She found Amelia in her office crying and wanted to take that bitch of a mother of hers down a few pegs.

"Amelia," Ryan said. "Sweetheart. She was just being a bitch because she was pissed off."

"I know. She's practically sent out the invitations. I just don't understand why she's insisting on this marriage when she knows it would be a disaster."

"Do you want to go through with it?"

"I'm not going through with it," she said firmly. "I'm even more determined to move on with my life."

"I'll be here to help any way I can."

"Thanks." Amelia hugged her. "You better go."

"Yeah." Ryan had the feeling Amelia would be gone by this time tomorrow after an evening of being emotionally beaten up and back into shape.

****

After Ryan was gone, Amelia went into the bathroom to wash her face. Then, back out into her office where her mother was waiting for her.

She studied her knowing what was coming.

"I'm ashamed of you Amelia," Felicia said coldly. "You've been nothing but a disappointment to me."

"I know."

"This is your only chance to get back in my good graces."

"How?"

"You'll go to Greg and apologize for your misstep and beg him to forgive you. Then, you'll accept his proposal, and the wedding will be in four months. You'll get part of your inheritance to set up your home, and you'll come to work at the foundation."

"No," Amelia said simply.

"No?" Felicia looked at her, confusion on her face. "You're not going to continue working at that library."

"No, I'm not, Mother," she said evenly. "I'm tired of being told where to go, who to see and how to dress. I'm tired of being treated like a possession, and Greg, he's not the man for me even if I wasn't gay."

"Greg knows you need a firm hand."

"I'm not a child. I need a partner not someone who wants to manhandle me. He's hit me more than once when he's had too much to drink, and I will not consign myself to a life of occasional abuse be it physical, mental, or emotional."

"I'm sure you deserved it," her mother retorted. "You're always stepping out of line."

"I want you to get out of my office, Mother," Amelia said acidly.

"If you refuse to do this, I'll never speak to you again."

"Fine by me," Amelia told her. "You won't have anything to say to me that's worth hearing anyway." She walked over to her desk and picked up the phone. Amelia hit a button. "Yes, this is Amelia, Ray."

"Hello, Miss Rose-Brier. What can I do for you?"

"Can you have security come to my office and escort Mrs. Allen and her guest out?"

"Right away," he said congenially.

"Thank you."

Her mother stared at her in rapt disbelief. "You'll never have anything, and she won't stay without the money because you're a weak sniveling idiot."

"Then, when I get up and drag myself into my bathroom every morning, I'll be able to look myself in the eye and be content with the woman I am and the decisions I've made."

"You think—" Her mother broke off at the rap on the door.

"Come in," Amelia called, and the door opened.

"Amelia," Greg said. "What have you been telling that woman?" he demanded stalking in, glowering at her.

"Not half of what I will be telling her now that I'm free of you two," she responded in an even tone that surprised her. "I'm not a whore to be auctioned off to the highest bidder. I know you're both getting something out of me being with Greg's family. I also know that whatever it is, won't benefit me any."

"As my wife—"

"I will never be your anything Greg," Amelia told him. "I came here to get away from you both. After the way you treated me that night, I knew—"

"What are you talking about?" Felicia demanded.

"He tried to rape me, Mother," Amelia snapped. "He hit me, and then tried to rape me because I refused to have sex with him. And last year, he broke my arm when I tried to get away from him."

"I had too much to drink, Amelia," he muttered. "I told you I'd get help."

"I don't care if you don't," she rebutted. "You're not my problem anymore, Greg."

There was a rap on her door, and it opened. Framed in it was a tall man with dark brown hair and gray eyes. "Miss Rose-Brier?"

"Ray, please escort these people from my office and the building."

"This is part mine," Felicia told her coldly. "You can't throw me out of my own property."

"Felicia," Genny said and maneuvered around the security guard. "I think you and your guest and Grace need to leave my home. You're welcome to take rooms here at the inn."

"Genny—"

"I've had your bags brought over," she said. "Ray, escort them out of the office area to their rooms unless they're leaving."

"You'll regret this, Amelia." Felicia sneered at her and breezed from the room with Greg on her heels.

"He's hit you?" her aunt asked closing the door.

"Yes, and I know I'm—I just have no excuses for allowing myself to be in that position. My therapist said I should try harder and be less of a complainer."

"A therapist told you that?"

She laughed bitterly. "Mother recommended her. She said it was for my sexual dysfunction, but it was really to beat me down and try and make me straight. I stopped seeing her after he broke my arm."

"What? Who broke your arm?"

She shook her head, swallowing tightly. "Greg. Last year. I wouldn't have sex with him, and he grabbed me. I tried to get away and he attacked me and broke my arm. Grandmother came to the hospital, and she told me to keep quiet. I couldn't ruin his life because I was frigid."

"Amelia—"

"It wasn't all the time," she said. "He just got drunk and when he did, I made sure I wasn't alone with him. Otherwise, he was nice or just condescending. He thought my work at the library was unimportant and so did Grandmother and Mother."

Genny hugged her. "Amelia."

"I've been in therapy. Trust me I know what part of this is my fault." She sighed, backing away from her aunt. "And I'm not going back to that."

Her aunt moved in to give her a hug. "I didn't know you were so unhappy."

She shrugged. "I'm putting it behind me."

"As you should. "Amelia?"

"Yes?"

"Did he just almost rape you?"

"He never raped me," she said. "I would have filed charges. But it's all over with now. I'm done being a prisoner in my own life."

"Does this have anything to do with Ryan?" Her aunt asked.

"When you asked me to come here, I had already decided to come down for a few days to think. Your invitation only made it that much easier to get out of there. Coming here was the best thing I've done in years."

"And if Ryan doesn't want anything serious or real?"

"She does, but we might not be each other's one, but I'm staying here." She shrugged. "I'm home."

Chapter Sixteen

"Ryan, where have you been?" Evers demanded two hours after she got back to work.

Ryan gave him a confused look as she halted her stride into her office. "What do you mean? I took lunch at one, and I've been back here for two hours working."

"My nephew said he waited in your office for you for the last two hours and you were MIA."

She snorted. "The kid never came here," she said. "I need to finish up this paperwork."

"Where did you go for lunch? The inn?"

"Yes."

She studied him watching his expression change. "You were over there screwing around instead of here."

"Last I checked I get an hour lunch," she told him. "I ate and I was back here in forty-five minutes."

"My nephew doesn't have a reason to lie."

"Yeah, he does, but it's not my problem," she told him.

"You're fired."

"Fine," she said. "I take it you have my check ready? If not, I'll pick it up in the morning."

"I—"

"I know my rights," she cut in. "I don't have to wait until pay day since you terminated me."

"I'll mail it to you."

"No. I'll pick it up in the morning," she insisted.

"Ryan—Fine," he said.

"I'll grab my stuff," Ryan replied. She turned away from him and headed to her office. His nephew was seated behind her desk fiddling with her computer. "Get out of my chair you little phisher," she ordered. "This is your office when I finish up in ten minutes."

"It's my office now," he told her with a smug smile.

"Get out of my chair, or I'll go to the bank's owner and tell him you were trying to steal files and embezzle funds on your first day."

He stared at her, his expression hardening. "He won't believe you."

"Maybe, but if any money comes up missing, plus the fact that you're in my office messing with my computer after lying about me, won't look good."

He got out of her chair, and Ryan readjusted the height.

"Wait outside, please," Ryan told him.

"I—

"It's still my office until I walk out, so beat it, kid," she ordered, and he held her gaze for a long moment before exiting, grumbling under his breath.

Ryan closed the door in his face and sat down. She input her password and sent all of her files to her supervisor leaving nothing on her computer for him to look at. She then, locked the computer. Then, Ryan unlocked the desk drawer and removed her tablet computer and its case.

She put them on her desk before removing some papers. She did some quick work on her tablet and then closed and locked it. After that, Ryan put the device in its case and got to her feet.

Ryan was about to open the door when it opened. Her colleague Rodney stood there.

"Ryan, I need to talk to you a minute," he said.

"Sure, but I don't have more than that. Evers just fired me."

He glanced over his shoulder at the young man holding up the wall. "For that know nothing? Barker better stop him before he has him in hot water with the FDIC."

"Well, I can't say I'd care either way. Barker is no friend of mine," she said, thinking of their boss and owner of the bank.

"Could you take a look at this before you go?"

She took the file he handed her. Ryan took her time going over it. "I sent Michael all my files."

"Could have been the wrong move," he told her shaking his head. "Do you have the SD?"

"Yeah, I was going to run that by his office."

"Can I have it?"

"Sure." Ryan picked the card up from her desk. She backed up all her files on SDs that she regularly updated to prevent loss of data in the event of a system failure.

"Thanks," he said. "I appreciate it. What are you going to do?"

"I already have a job," she said.

"Rena. I'm surprised you held on this long. Good luck."

"Yeah, thanks. I'll be doing some part time work for Miss Genny too until she can hire a new business manager."

"Great for her," he said. "I heard you were seeing her niece."

"That's true."

Rodney nodded. "Well, good luck, and I'll see you around."

"Later, man." She bumped fists with him and grabbed her tablet. He exited ahead of her, and Ryan followed him out. She was glad to have this place in her past.

She got in her truck and drove over to the inn. Miss Genny was in her office talking to the police. She motioned Ryan in.

"Hi, Ryan," Detective Morris said. "Miss Genny was just telling me you handled the audit that revealed the discrepancies."

"I did," she agreed.

"We arrested Leah this morning," he said. "I'll need a copy of your findings."

"I have that right here," Miss Genny told him. "Ryan gave me the file."

"Okay, great," he said. "Ryan I'll need to talk to you as things progress."

"I'll be here," she answered.

"If things are in order, it'll be an open and shut case," Detective Morris told them. "Kilpatrick is already saying he'd offer her a plea deal."

"Is that appropriate for the A.D.A to be talking to her so soon?" Miss Genny asked.

"He talked to her this morning," Detective Morris replied. "He just wants to get things handled before the holidays start rolling in."

"As long as she's punished. She stole over a hundred thousand dollars from me."

"I understand," he said. "We'll have to see what happens."

"I did trace the money to an offshore account," Ryan informed him. "I included my notes on the route it took. I think someone else is involved and that someone is probably someone who works here or lives in town."

"We'll look into it," he replied. "Can I see her office? Maybe she left some traces there of who her partner is."

"Yes, by all means," Miss Genny said. "I'll show you. Ryan, did you want to see me about something?"

"I came to tell you I can start tomorrow."

"No. I want you to take Amelia to the city. So, she can get things handled there."

"Okay. I can leave when she's ready."

"Go talk to her. She's in her office."

"I'll see you when I get back," Ryan said.

"Okay. You can fill out your paperwork before you leave today and when Leah's office is released, you can take it. In the meantime, take the one next to Amelia's."

"Okay."

"I'll have it cleaned while you're gone, and I'll give you a key when you return."

"Yes, ma'am," she said. Ryan left the office and went to find Amelia. She was in her office looking more relaxed than Ryan had ever seen her. "Hi, sweetheart."

"Hey. Do you think you could take me to the city today? I don't really have a lot that I'm going to be bringing back."

"What's the hurry?"

"I want to get back there today because my mother is probably furious. Aunt Genny threw her out. She'll go there and mess with my stuff or have me locked out of my apartment so I can't get the few things I'd like."

"Sure. We can leave whenever you're ready."

"Great because I'm ready now."

"Okay," Ryan said. "Then, let's hit the road."

"Give me ten?"

"Sure. I'll hang out in the dining room and have a cup of coffee."

"You don't have to," she said. "I'm just finishing up a few things on my computer. I'm going to send my aunt a message to let her know we're leaving."

"Okay."

Ryan took a seat in front of Amelia's desk and pulled out her phone. She found a message from Mihai and dialed his number as she got up and headed out of Amelia's office.

"Hello?"

"Hi Uncle Mihai," she said. "I got your message."

"You didn't have to call, Ryan," he said tiredly.

"I'm sorry," she said. "You were probably sleeping."

"I was just finishing up some work," he told her. "I just wanted to make sure you got the information. Everything is set. There are one or two others who are thinking of joining your coven. Children of some of the court who wish to relocate."

"Oh?"

"You've met them at one time or another though it might have been years since."

"Send me names and pictures so I can start getting my head around it."

He chuckled. "One of them lives right there in town. Bailey Mikkelsen."

"The baker," Ryan said. She'd known Bailey since they were kids.

"The other one you haven't seen since your mother's funeral, but he's a good kid who just want a quiet life in a small town."

"Okay," she said. "They're welcome."

"We'll finalize things when I get back," Mihai told her. "Go ahead and check on that account, I want you to make sure everything is in order. Your father was a quirky, almost old-fashion kind of man in some cases."

"Where women are concerned."

"Yes. Your sexuality wouldn't shock him. In fact, he had one request on that. I'll be speaking to you about it when I return."

"Okay. I'll check out the account. What do you want me to do with it?"

"Whatever you want," he said, his tone almost puzzled. "It's your inheritance. Your father left you a few other things which I'll be bringing back. Until then."

"See you later, Uncle Mihai." She ended the call and checked the information he'd sent her before pulling up the account.

Ryan stared at the numbers and almost choked on her own spittle.

"I'm ready," Amelia said.

Ryan glanced at her. "Yeah." She logged out of the account. "Let's ride then." She got to her feet and followed Amelia to the door.

They made their way out to the parking lot and climbed into Ryan's truck and got on the road. The drive was a quiet one. The conversation light and infrequent. Ryan didn't mind, her thoughts were on her parents and the fortune her father had bequeathed her.

That letter he'd left her had spoken of her father's love for her and his wish for her to be happy in her choice of career. He also expressed a hope that she lived each moment like the sun would incinerate her tomorrow.

He wanted her to find love and embrace her life, embrace his world when she turned 35 at least. Thinking about it now, Ryan wished he could be here with her. She wished both her parents were here, but she was thankful for the man who'd loved and cared for her.

They made it to the city an hour later and it took another twenty minutes to get to Amelia's apartment. The complex was a gated one and Amelia told her the code to open the gate.

Ryan drove through the complex to Amelia's unit. Once inside, Amelia sighed. Ryan looked around taking in the colors and smell.

It was clear everything cost a fortune. She recognized the artwork, the furniture. She had a piece by the artist in her own home, but her life was more about comfort and function than fashion.

What she didn't see in the well put together place was Amelia.

Only the splash of soft pastel in the throw pillows and the magazine on the coffee suggested Amelia lived here.

"You hired a decorator?" Ryan asked.

"My mother did," she answered. "The place had to look a certain way for when I had people over."

"Your friends."

"I don't have any actual friends, Ryan," she replied quietly. "The women that came over were a book club that my mother insisted I join. They were women from the foundation my grandmother runs."

"What kind of books do you guys read?"

She shrugged. "We recently read Michelle Obama's book and before that some books on money, saving it, investing it. Some of them are really nice and interested in their retirement."

"Not you?"

"We agreed to do an investment account and pick some stocks and stuff. I made a little money for my Roth."

Ryan nodded. "You know it is important to take an interest in your retirement fund."

Amelia laughed. "I used to think so." She looked away.

"But now?"

Amelia shook her head. "I already called my boss," Amelia said changing the subject. "Since my mother claims, he didn't want to hire me, there's no need for me to give him the courtesy of going by and doing it in person."

"What about the super?"

"My mom is renting the apartment because where I lived wasn't upscale enough," Amelia said and led the way from the room. "So, I just need to get my clothes and a few things that are actually mine. She bought everything because what I had wasn't good enough to be seen by her friends' daughters."

"Ah." Ryan followed in Amelia's wake.

They ended up in her bedroom, a spacious room with a large bed simply draped and canopy curtains on either side that gave the room a relaxed and yet slightly romantic look.

The twin night tables were in cherry wood just like the sleigh bed and the curtains were layered. The gauzy soft pastel curtains draped over sheers with a pretty fabric topper.

The dressing table held the usual items with a single candle and a statue of Bastet which made Ryan smile.

She turned her gaze on Amelia who had a suitcase open on the bed now and several items from a drawer thrown into it. Ryan took in the scent of the room, smiling again.

"Vanilla."

"I love the smell of it," Amelia said.

She could tell by the candles everywhere. A single red one was mixed in, and Ryan detected the slightest hint of cinnamon.

Amelia went to the closet and removed a second bag. She put it on the bed and opened it. She went back to the closet for more items and put them in the bag before going back to the dresser.

Ryan picked up one of the books. It was an old leather-bound text. She opened it and paged through it.

A kitchen witch's book of shadows. Some of the recipes had changes and they all had hand drawn pictures.

"Have you ever used any of these?" Ryan asked continuing to look through the book.

"Is that the cookbook?"

"Yeah."

"I've used some," she said.

"Have you written any in here?"

"Two," Amelia admitted with a furtive glance and Ryan smiled. "It was my great-grandmother's. She left it to me when she passed away. Two other books came with it. She didn't think anyone else in the family could appreciate them."

Ryan picked up one of the other books. She thumbed through it. "These are fantastic, Amelia. Have you made them?"

"No, what are they?" she asked.

"Like this one, no more roughing it. It's a foot cream. Your great granny was a cottage witch."

"I—Maybe."

"Oh, look at this, she made her own perfume too."

"Really?" Amelia asked. "I've never even looked through that one."

"I guess you've got some interesting reading ahead of you," Ryan commented.

"Sounds like it," she said.

"Were those cookies magic cookies?" Ryan teased. "I ate every last one."

Amelia laughed. "No. Don't be silly."

Ryan put down the book and went to kiss the back of Amelia's neck. She wrapped her arms around Amelia and nipped the side of her neck.

Amelia shivered and the energy in the room shifted slightly. Amelia's scent changed a little, became more enticing. Ryan stepped away from her and Amelia threw her a look over her shoulder, her eyes vivid green.

Ryan smiled and went to lean against the wall next to the dresser. Amelia tracked her, slowly following her movement. There was a seductress inside her shy pretty baby.

Amelia tore her gaze from her and began to pack again. Ryan watched her go through a jewelry box and leave what looked like pricy pieces behind.

"Why are you leaving those?"

"My mother bought them. She'll want them back. Her goal right now is to strip me of everything she thinks is important including expensive jewelry and clothes."

She moved to the closet and came out with a few items. Amelia folded them and put them in the suitcase before grabbing a bag and adding shoes. Then, Amelia went into the bathroom and returned with an overnight bag. She set it on the bed and removed everything from the nightstand drawer and closed it.

"I have a laptop in the spare room and that's about it."

"That's it?"

"Yeah." Amelia nodded, glancing around.

"Won't take long to load these in my truck," Ryan said.

"Great. Then, we can get back by dinner," Amelia replied. She looked around the apartment.

"There is nothing wrong with not wanting to give all this up."

"Yes, it is," she said firmly. "I can't have better if I stay here." Amelia shrugged.

"Amelia, can I ask you something about Greg?"

Amelia met her gaze. "Sure."

"Did he ever get rough with you?" Ryan asked. "Hit you."

She nodded and looked away. "I could say it was mostly my fault—"

"It would be a lie," Ryan said angrily. "No woman is ever to blame for a man abusing her be it physical, mental, or emotional. You're worth better."

"Did your dad teach you that?"

"Yeah." Ryan went to her and pulled her into a hug. "You're making the right decision to get away from him."

"I should have done it sooner," Amelia said. "But it's better late than never."

"That's true."

Amelia nodded and rested her hands on Ryan's shoulders, linking them around her neck. "My aunt said it was okay for me to have company, and I was thinking I wouldn't be alone in my wing some nights."

"I'd be more than happy to keep you company," Ryan told her.

"Good because I think that's what girlfriends do," she said shyly. "Especially, when one doesn't want to be alone."

Ryan laughed. "You're cute, you know that?"

"I don't have that much experience, I know," she said. "You probably think—"

"You're cute is what I think," Ryan broke in and dipped her head and kissed Amelia.

Amelia sighed into the kiss, pressing against Ryan. Ryan's arms went around her. She could virtually feel Amelia's need to be held, and she was more than happy to oblige.

Ryan backed them up so her back rested against the wall next to the dresser. She drew her hands down and Amelia arched into her, her body rippling against her enticingly.

She drew her hands over Amelia's ass, squeezed. Amelia's soft fingers caressed her nape. Ryan didn't want to get too deep into this given this was unfamiliar territory, but Amelia felt so good against her, so right.

She had a hard time resisting her, so she knew this was going to go a little further.

"Ryan," Amelia murmured, and Ryan's lips brushed against the side of her mouth. The scent of Amelia already going to her head.

Ryan trailed kisses along the side of Amelia's neck to where shoulder and neck met. As she did so, she unbuttoned her blouse. Sharp teeth nipped before soft lips firmed and sucked at her succulent flesh.

Damn she had to have a little taste of her.

****

"Mmm." Amelia pushed a hand into the thick strands of Ryan's hair as she strained closer to her. "Ryan," Amelia murmured, tipping her head back, exposing her throat.

Ryan's lips skimmed over the lean column. Her tongue swirled in the hollow at its base and Amelia shivered.

Ryan's fingers slid between Amelia's legs, and Amelia creamed her panties as her clit hardened. Ryan released the button of Amelia's pants and pushed her hand inside to run her fingers up the damp slit to the swollen nubbin of her clit.

Amelia gasped, pleasure rushing her like a tidal wave crashing to shore. "Ryan, I need..." She needed her in the worst way. She could barely put into words how much she ached for her touch.

Ryan sucked Amelia's throat as she pushed her fingers past the band of Amelia's panties. Amelia's breath came out in rough pants as slim fingers whispered over her clit. Her hips jerked, and she cried out, the sound needy and desperate.

Ryan's thumb pressed against her clitoris while two fingers tested the readiness of her pussy. Sliding in through the sticky juices, Ryan's fingers penetrated the tight cavern.

"Yes," Amelia moaned, her body catching fire. She gripped Ryan's shoulder tight, rolling her hips attempting to drive Ryan's fingers deeper into her wet depths.

Ryan pressed her thumb more firmly against Amelia's clit and fucked her with rough strokes.

"Oh God!" Amelia mewled as Ryan took her faster, driving her fingers in, fucking her like a woman who knew how to take possession of a woman's body.

Amelia's eyes slid closed as the heat of pleasure rolled over her, stealing her breath.

"Damn, your body knows it belongs to me," Ryan murmured, and Amelia's eyes fluttered open. Their gazes locked and the possession in those dark eyes should have frightened her. Instead, it turned her on, made her want Ryan even more.

Never had anyone looked at her like that before or made her feel so wanted. Some alien part of her just came alive right then and filled every inch of her mind.

Her body seemed weightless, her thoughts not quite her own, but the passion grew stronger, the heat of her skin almost intense.

Ryan crooked her fingers and found that spot. She stroked it, and Amelia came undone. She put a hand on Ryan's, her nails digging in. She was so close.

The smell of her, the sound of her heart beating and the strong vibration of her energy—It was almost musical. Amelia wanted to—needed to taste her to—She dug her nails in deeper on instinct and a rush of energy inundated her. She threw her head back sucking it in. She couldn't stop, she was hungry for it.

"Ryan, my goddess, don't stop!" She screamed, the delectation too much.

Ryan pulled her fingers out and thrust them back in, and Amelia cried out, her body pulling tight. Her head spun as she came, the orgasm closing around her, a tight grip.

Ryan's lips were soft on her throat as they moved to her neck. The slight prick barely registered. That strange part of her sighed. The heady rush of pleasure was almost too much.

Amelia let out a breathless scream unable to contain the energy of her release.

Trembling, she struggled to hold onto the moment, but darkness came over her and she sagged in Ryan's arms.

****

Ryan retracted her fangs, sated yet energized. She held Amelia against her, bracing one hand on the wall. Amelia had fed from her, and it had been as erotic as sex itself.

This was definitely a game changer.

She had thought Mihai was wrong about Amelia, but this was the second time Amelia had fed from her, energetically. But that made her no less one of them. However, this time had been no accident. Amelia had known what she'd needed and taken it.

This had been her true awakening and technically, she'd sired Amelia since she'd activated the change. This would be her seventeenth and most delicious.

She hadn't brought anyone across without thought except the first four times. Those had been accidents. The others had been intentional. They'd been left to die or dying. She had been selective in her college years and time in New York.

She'd headed her own coven there with a house of fourteen including Ree.

Ryan had tasted all of the pleasure of being a vampire. If she was honest, it was the only area of her life in New York that had given her satisfaction after a time. However, she had been unwilling to stay for that alone.

Amelia stirred against her, and Ryan's thoughts immediately went to her, her gaze going to Amelia as her lashes fluttered up. Her eyes were a vivid green before fading to their Jade shade.

Amelia reached up to caress Ryan's jaw. "Let me please you."

"Next time," Ryan murmured. "Just getting you off was enough for me." And for now, it was.

"Ryan, you're incredible. You make me feel…"

"Incredible?" Ryan asked in a teasing tone. Yeah, she bet she did feel incredible. Someone was going to have to talk to her. Ryan hoped that wasn't her, but it was clear why Miss Genny had wanted Amelia in Avon Del.

"More than that." Amelia looked away. "I should clean up."

Ryan didn't move. She kept her pinned in place until Amelia met her gaze again.

"You're safe with me Amelia," Ryan told her gently. "Whoever you are deep down inside is okay with me." Ryan kissed the corner of her mouth.

Amelia nodded slowly. "Thanks."

"I'll take your things out to the truck," Ryan said drawing away from her. "Take your time." Ryan dropped a kiss on her forehead. "Where's your bathroom?"

"Over there." Amelia pointed.

Ryan crossed the room to the bathroom. It was spacious and neatly ordered. Nothing that gave too much idea of Amelia's personality unless you counted the shelf on the wall that reminded her of a wall altar.

Ryan washed her hands thinking Amelia had managed to save a small piece of herself from her family. Now, all she had to do was let that small light shine.

Chapter Seventeen

Alone now, Amelia considered what had happened moments ago with Ryan. She tried to get her mind around it, wondering why she'd felt the overpowering hunger.

She'd felt that hunger all day. It had merely intensified with each hour until she'd been powerless to stop it.

Stop it?

Stop what?

What had happened? She didn't really understand any of it—not the way part of her had merely turned off and another part had taken over. That part had siphoned energy from Ryan, taken hard pulls. The rush had been intoxicating and overwhelming.

She could still take more, but the edge was gone. Amelia pushed the fear and concern—had she been bitten by something that was changing her?

Not Ryan. Ryan was...human not some animal. Not a bat or a werewolf that could change her.

She laughed nervously.

"Listen to you," she whispered. "Talking like this is some old vampire movie." She shoved the thought to the back of her mind. She didn't know what had happened and right now she only wanted to deal with one emotional thing at a time.

So, Amelia went into the bathroom to clean up. Then, she took one last look around. There were some positive memories here, but most were of a young woman who'd spent years hiding her true self for fear of losing things she doubted she ever really had.

Like so many times, Amelia wondered what it was about her that had made her so unlovable. Maybe she reminded her mother and grandmother too much of the man who'd walked away from his wife.

She didn't know anything about her father, but she would love to. She'd been young when he'd left, and her mother never spoke about him.

Or maybe it was the magic.

Her grandmother had taken great pangs to ensure no mention of it ever made it into the family even when her great-grandmother, her grandmother's mother had been alive.

Amelia retrieved her phone from the dresser and dialed her grandmother's number. However, those journals proved witchcraft had roots in her family.

And the amulet that kept her safe from the severe burns of the sun.

"Hello?"

"Hello Grandmother," she said demurely. "How are you?"

"Hello, Amelia," she answered coolly. "I've spoken with your mother and Grace. They've both told me you've taken up with a female hick."

Amelia almost laughed. "I am seeing a woman. Her name is Ryan," Amelia said.

"A woman with a boy's name?" she demanded, disdain in her voice. "What do you want?"

"I want to know about my father," she said. "Who is he? Where is he?"

"He was worthless. He left your mother with no hint of where he was going."

"He never paid child support?"

"He paid for your education and clothing, but nothing more," she retorted. "That was the agreement. Why?"

"I'd like to find him," she answered honestly. Maybe he was a witch too. Amelia didn't have any hope of a relationship with the man, but maybe he could share his family's heritage of witchcraft with her.

"Don't waste your time, but then you are very like him in that you're as thoughtless as he is. He didn't give a moment's thought to what would happen to the family if he just left."

"What's his name?" she asked.

"Maybe if you find him, he'll offer you some financial assistance now that you won't have your inheritance."

"You never intended to allow me to have it, did you?" she asked softly.

"You're a disgrace to this family, Amelia," her grandmother replied. "And now that you've taken up with some gay hick you've forfeited."

"You're in financial trouble and marrying me off didn't take so you need my inheritance to dig out of a hole." The realization slammed into her so hard she had to catch her breath.

Not only that, but they were also probably going to siphon off her inheritance after giving her only a small portion.

"You're very smart Amelia just like Genevieve. Don't contact me or anyone else in the family anymore. None of us will have anything to do with you unless you come crawling back and do as you're told."

"I'll never allow you or Mother to treat me like a second-class citizen again," Amelia told her coldly. "I'd rather never speak to any of you again."

"Good because as of now your wish is granted."

"I have just one more question," Amelia said.

"Which is?" The acid in those words could have burned.

"Was great-grandmother a practicing witch?"

The silence was telling.

"My mother was a heretic just like her aunt. No doubt they'll both burn in hell as will you if you won't straighten your life up and leave the devil's house."

"I won't be burning in hell alone, Grandmother," she murmured.

Suddenly nothingness filled her ear, and she closed her eyes and drew in a breath and slowly let it out. She'd wasted so many years of her life being unhappy. At least now it was over.

She was free to explore who Amelia Rose-Brier was. Today was the first day of the rest of her life.

****

"Thank you for letting me see her, Alvin," Genny said to the police chief.

"It's not a problem, but I don't think you're going to find the answers you're looking for. She's considering taking the plea, but she hasn't agreed to."

"Could I drop the charges?"

"I'd do it as a personal favor," he said. "But I wouldn't advise it."

She nodded. "I'll see what she has to say. Maybe she has a good reason."

"Your call."

The door of the conference room opened, and the brunette was brought in. She wasn't cuffed as they often were on TV. Leah was wearing the orange jumpsuit and her lovely face was devoid of makeup.

She had the true look of her mother. Genny frowned. She'd known her late husband's longest lasting affair quite well. Delia had been a poor woman from a small family. Both sisters had always been trying to snare a man of means rather than better themselves.

That Delia had been a maid hadn't prevented her and Genny from becoming friends. Their friendship had begun to fall apart shortly after Genny's husband's realization that he was broke.

Around that same time, Delia had gotten pregnant with her second child. Leah had only been three.

Genny remembered the snickers behind her back and the sly comments that she couldn't have children. She also recalled the smug look on Delia's face each time she saw her.

It was always as if she had a secret. Even after Genny's husband's death, Delia had acted as if she had something that Genny would never have.

But Delia had moved away a few months after the second child was born.

Leah's eyes were those of her mother, gray, filled with smugness.

"Hello, Leah," she said.

"Genevieve."

"You look so much like your mother," Genny murmured. "When I first met you, you reminded me how she was when I met her."

Delia had been full of life with a head for numbers. She'd been generous and the kind of friend Genny had wanted her whole life.

"Who am I?" she demanded. "You have no idea. "You're so wrapped up in your own life like all rich people."

She smiled faintly. Genny had hired the sisters because she'd wanted to give them the chance at a decent job their mother had always seemed to crave but had never gotten. She'd helped them behind the scenes in securing a nice home thinking they'd deserved a chance and perhaps their mother would have made better choices had someone given her the same opportunity.

"You're Delia Everlast's daughter. My husband's oldest child. He was the self-absorbed one." Genny wondered if he'd even loved Delia or if she'd just been a balm to his wounded ego.

"He wasn't like that. He loved us," she said coldly. "And my mother died because of you."

"Me?"

"She was dying of cancer, and you wouldn't lift a finger to help her, to help us," Leah growled. "I took what's rightfully ours."

"What do you think that is?" Genny asked carefully.

"The inn, all the money," she said. "It's Addy and mine's inheritance."

"Your mother told you this?"

"Yes. So did my aunt."

"He lied to your mother," Genny replied on a sigh. "You came to work for me in order to steal from me on a lie." She laughed.

"It wasn't a lie," Leah screamed as she slapped her hand on the table. "The inn belongs to us. Every dime you've made off it belongs to us."

"The land the inn is on belongs to my family," Genny told her evenly. "The people you should have been trying to milk are the Fords. Your father's family, but they went broke. When they did, your father couldn't stand it. None of them could really. Half of them started down paths of destruction that led to their eventual deaths."

"You're lying."

"Bad investments, mismanagement of their businesses, and extravagance by the majority of them ate up their money. When it was gone, your father tried to steal mine. He slowly siphoned off money for himself and your mother before he was killed in a car accident."

"He couldn't steal what was his."

"What was mine was never his," Genny told her. "He had to sign a pre-nuptial agreement. It was part of my mother's will to prevent me from being fleeced by some man marrying me for my assets. A divorce would have gotten him nothing, but we were headed for that. I had grown tired of his cheating."

The girl stared at her. Shock, horror and then plain rage filled her face.

"That's not true. My mother and my aunt said the inn was ours and all the money. She said you knew we were hungry and refused to give us so much as a dime."

"I didn't know about your situation. I would have helped because there was a time when I loved your father and your mother had been a very close friend of mine. I would have welcomed a renewal of our friendship."

"If you mean that, drop the charges," Leah commanded.

"I'm not going to do that," Genny told her. "You stole from me and lied to my face. Now, you act like you're due what was never yours. Though I would have given you something because of what your parents once meant to me."

"Then, do it instead of acting like a greedy bitch."

Genny got to her feet, a hint of anger swirling in her belly. "You remind me of him," she said with a ghost of a smile. "And Delia, you do look so much like her. Addy though, she looks more like your grandmother."

"Leave Addy alone."

"Why, she helped you." She shrugged. "I'm sure she even has part of the money. She'll need it for your defense. Alvin." She moved to the door not wanting to be anywhere near the young woman any longer.

The door opened and a guard stepped in.

"Do whatever you want to me, but Addy had nothing to do with this," she screamed. "You owe us!"

"I owe you nothing, Leah." She walked out, the guard grabbed Leah who tried to grab her as she did so.

"Well?" Alvin asked.

"Could you reduce the charges to petty theft or something?"

"If you like," he said. "You came to me. You can say the audit was in error."

"That'll be fine."

"I can reduce the jail time to one to three years in a plea deal with her serving maybe six months."

"Have you arrested Addy yet?"

"A little while ago," he said. "They picked her up at the inn. The info your guy gave us helped us track the money, and Addy did use some of it to open an account at a bank in Pine Del."

The town next to theirs.

"I don't have any proof Addy was involved so you could just let her go," Genny murmured. "She might have just won that money at a casino."

Alvin gave her a curious look. "Why the change of heart?" Alvin asked pulling her back as the cop brought Leah out."

Leah glared at her. "Selfish bitch," she muttered.

"Stop your whining, girl," the lieutenant said and tugged her away.

"I knew her father," she said.

Alvin nodded, understanding in his gaze. "I'll call her lawyer and make the proposal."

"Let me know what she decides."

"I will."

She exited the courthouse with a sigh. Naturally, Genny would be firing Addy. There was no way she could keep her on knowing the girl would likely cause trouble for Amelia once Genny was gone.

Her ex's children weren't going to cause her anymore trouble.

"How did it go?" Alston asked when she reached her car. He'd parked next to her.

"He led them to believe everything I had was his."

Alston sighed. "He was hurting bad," he said. "He couldn't handle being broke, and he knew you were on the verge of divorcing him."

"Do you think he was planning to kill me?"

"He might have been," Alston replied. I think he might have thought with you dead he could inherit your estate."

"He couldn't have," she murmured. "Everything I had was going to be split between my sister and her children including the inn."

"I don't think he knew that," Alston commented. "What are you going to do?"

"I had Alvin change the charges. She can keep the money she stole, and I'll give her sister a similar amount. That will be the end of it as far as I'm concerned."

"I'll have Barrett draw up the trust papers."

"Thank you. Have you been able to find out anything about my sister and stepmother's finances?"

"A very little," he said. "I have a woman on it. She's only learned there are whispers of mismanagement of the foundation's funds."

Her father had started the foundation her stepmother and half-sister now ran.

"She thinks they're going broke, and in heavy debt."

"That's why Amelia can't have her inheritance. They're going to use it to pay off debts."

"Maybe. I'll continue to look into things," Alston told her.

"And keep me updated?" Genny asked though she knew she didn't need to.

"Naturally." He nodded.

"Amelia is awakening," she said in so low a voice only another vampire or wolf shifter could have heard her.

"How can you tell?" he asked in a volume that matched her own.

"Her amulet is visible. She asked me about it and I told her part of the truth. Plus, Ryan bit her."

Alston exhaled. "She's feeding from her. Is there any indication from Mihai that she's ever fed before? She could be just awakening herself. If she is, she's dangerous."

"Amelia isn't the first," Genny answered. "She's brought over at least four that he and the Council knows of."

"You're going to have to tell Amelia," Alston murmured. "You should have told her sooner."

"There was no proof she'd ever change," she said defensively. "And if not for Ryan biting her, she might not have."

"True, so talk to Ryan Queen to Queen."

She snorted. "She's not a real queen. She's only sired—"

"Technically she is Amelia's sire since she could have stayed dormant forever," Alston broke in gently. "But given that Amelia isn't showing any signs of anemia or any hungers, it means Ryan hasn't taken much. She's in full control."

"Meaning she's been full on for a while," Genny muttered and shook her head. "I never wanted to have to tell Amelia about her father. I always assumed he'd be around if the time came."

"Then, you were going to bring her fully across?" he asked curiously.

"I was going to put her in the situation where someone of my coven did," she admitted looking down. It wasn't the best way to handle things, but she hadn't brought Amelia here purely for altruistic purposes.

She was only moderately ashamed of that.

"Honey."

"I have no children, Al," she said softly. "Amelia has to carry on my legacy. My mother wanted it."

"Your mother?"

"I'm not insane," she muttered. "I make no claims to having spoken with her ghost. She left specific instructions that my firstborn daughter take over the coven when it was time for me to move on. Everything connected with her legacy goes to my daughter."

"And by coven law Amelia is yours since her mother is your kin and you were partially involved in her upbringing."

"She's family." She shrugged. "My mother left very specific instructions for both case scenarios. The event that I had no children and the event of a child like Amelia being born into the family. I never wanted her father with her mother."

"But it's a lucky break that he ignored you."

"As it turns out."

Alston captured her hand. "Tell her before she finds out the wrong way. The full transformation could come slowly or like a bullet train. She'll be terrified of the thirst."

"I know."

"And goodness forbid Ryan should introduce her to our world by feeding her."

"I know. I'll tell her soon."

"Sooner rather than later, my love," Alston insisted.

"Tonight. Same time. Same place." They could talk about this some more and decide on the best course of action.

He smiled. "I can't wait." Alston opened her door for her, and she climbed into her car.

Her driver walked the short distance to the vehicle and got in. Genny looked out of the window holding Alston's gaze.

Tomorrow she'd tell Amelia who and what she was. She'd tell her about her legacy.

Chapter Eighteen

"Thanks Ryan," Amelia said as she released her seatbelt. She glanced at her, catching her profile and smiling. The dreads fell around her face calling attention to the strong jaw.

"No thanks necessary."

Amelia nodded. Ryan's voice was quiet, her expression thoughtful.

"Are you okay?" Ryan asked.

"I'm gonna be," she answered.

"If there's anything I can do…"

Amelia reached across the seat and touched her arm. "You've already helped me so much, Ryan, and you'll never know how grateful I am."

Ryan put her hand on Amelia's and her eyes widened.

"I scratched you. I didn't mean to be so…" she trailed off at Ryan's quiet laughter.

"It's fine, sweetheart," she said. "It's nothing. Are we still on for that dessert?"

"Yes." Amelia smiled. "Come by around eight?"

"I'll be here."

"I'll bring your bags in and then head home." Ryan took her bags in and up to her bedroom. There, Ryan put them down on the floor, and Amelia gave her a smile.

"You're so sweet," Amelia said softly as she shook her head. "I've never known a woman like you, and I want to hold you hostage, so I'll have you close whenever I want you."

"You don't have to hold me hostage, baby," she murmured. "I'm here whenever you want me."

Amelia went to stand in front of her. "I don't just want you, Ryan. I need you."

Ryan drew Amelia to her. "I'm here, Amelia. I'm here." She hugged her. "Whenever you need me."

Amelia wrapped her arms around Ryan and cuddled against her. She closed her eyes and the sound of Ryan's heart seemed loud, but something else was louder. Amelia felt it pulsing, a life, a quiet vibrant part of Ryan, that all but begged for her to taste it.

To devour it.

Her skin warmed at the very thought and her mouth watered. Her throat was suddenly parched. Her breathing became shallow, and Amelia stepped back from her, her own heart pounding hard now.

"What's wrong?" Ryan murmured moving closer.

Amelia rubbed her throat, the need almost overpowering and she didn't know what it was. It was the need for food, but she wasn't hungry. No, it was the need for drink. That was it. She was thirsty.

"Ryan—" Her hand shook, but Ryan didn't stop in her advance in fact she merely backed her against the nearest wall.

"What do you need, Amelia?"

The question was so far away. She couldn't think, could barely even hear for the rushing of blood in her ears.

Ryan's lips were close to hers and she could feel the heat of her, the spark. Her thirst increased and Amelia leaned toward Ryan. The scent of her was incredible. It was like cinnamon and chocolate.

"Ry-Ryan," she said breathlessly. "I'm—" She was so hungry. Amelia glided her hand up Ryan's letting her hand rest on her forearm.

"Tell me," Ryan urged softly.

Instinct took over and Amelia's fingers pushed into Ryan's hair as she tipped her head up and their lips met. Ryan's lips were soft against hers and the kiss gentle.

The hunger was a wave that washed over her, and Amelia's lips parted just as her nails elongated against Ryan's skin. The kiss deepened and Amelia was inundated with the cinnamon and chocolate. It washed over her, filled her senses.

She tasted it, savored it as their tongues dueled. She needed more because a little just wasn't enough.

Ryan lifted her head and Amelia let out a little cry. She wasn't finished.

Then, it hit her, like rain drops. Energy pelted her and she took it in sucking each one up like a hungry duckling. She moaned and Ryan lowered her head. The sharpness at her neck was brief and followed by a deluge of cinnamon and chocolate.

"Ah." Her head rolled back against the wall as she drank her fill. Ryan licked over her throat, sucked, and Amelia tugged hard on her hair as she feasted.

The energy just kept coming, filling her up, making her wet.

"Ryan," she said in a seductive tone.

"A little more," Ryan murmured, and Amelia closed her eyes.

The deluge slowed to a trickle, and she sagged, sated.

Ryan picked her up and carried her to the bed and lay her on it before lying down next to her. Amelia rested her head on Ryan's shoulder even as she curled against her. She felt safe, wanted.

Amelia slowly came back to herself unsure what had happened. She had no idea what to say or how to explain it.

"Okay?" Ryan asked.

Amelia sat up, and Ryan pushed the curtain of red hair aside and kissed her nape.

Amelia smiled and moved more quickly than she ever had in her life, putting Ryan's back against the mattress and straddling her. There was surprise in Ryan's eyes, but she laughed.

Ryan sat up. "I guess you are."

Amelia kissed her as she wrapped one arm around Ryan's neck. Their tongues dueled in a caress that turned hot quickly. Desire clamped a hand around her and her nipples hardened.

Ryan's hands were on her back tugging her blouse from her pants so she could slip them beneath.

Amelia moaned. She moved against Ryan, feeling more daring than she'd ever felt.

"You want me?" Amelia asked.

"Oh, baby," Ryan murmured. "I could eat you alive."

"Prove it."

Ryan gave her a slow grin and ripped her blouse open and lowered her head to trace kisses over one creamy mound. She released the catch of Amelia's bra and buried her head between her breasts as her hands supported Amelia's back.

With her teeth, Ryan tugged the fabric aside and licked a pert nipple. She laved the tender flesh before sucking it into her mouth.

Heat rushed through Amelia, catching her on fire. She rubbed against Ryan, her clit engorged, the sensation electrifying.

"Amelia Amaia!" the harsh snap of her name was like cold water on the strengthening embers of desire.

"Shit," Amelia breathed and shuddered.

"I've got you, pretty baby," Ryan murmured as she lifted her head.

"What the hell is going on?" Felicia demanded.

"Mother," Amelia said in a chilled tone. "You are an unwelcome bucket of cold water. Get out."

"Get up Amelia," Felicia ordered.

"I said get out." She started to throw out her hand, but Ryan caught her off guard and rolled them.

Amelia was on her back and Ryan climbed out of bed.

"I'll head out," Ryan said. "Call me later if you change your mind."

"I'm not changing my mind," she said softly and climbed out of bed. Ryan held out a robe to her and Amelia took it. "Thanks." She leaned toward Ryan and Ryan kissed her.

"I'll see you later."

"Okay." Amelia smiled. She watched Ryan make a quick exit before turning her gaze on her mother.

"I can't believe you," Felicia said, disgust in her gaze.

"People have sex with their lovers all the time. You should know," Amelia said coolly.

Felicia's hand shot out and she struck her across the face. Amelia glared at her, the urge to kill her seizing her, but she walked past her instead as she pulled the robe on to cover her nakedness.

"Do you actually think having gay sex has given you a backbone enough to take me on?"

"I don't need one," Amelia told her, her tone distant. "What do you want?"

"I want you to get your ass back—"

"I'm not going," Amelia cut into her rant. "Now, leave me the hell alone before I call the police and have you arrested for assault."

Felicia stared at her in surprise. "Do you seriously think that two-bit hustler can help you?"

"I didn't ask Ryan for help," Amelia retorted. "And I don't actually need it at the moment. I just need you to leave."

"I'm not going anywhere without you," Felicia told her.

"Don't bet on that," Amelia growled.

"Amelia—" Felicia reached for her, and Amelia blocked the grab and shoved her mother.

"Don't you ever attempt to touch me again," Amelia told her acidly. "From now on, I'll be deciding what's best for me, not you."

Shocked, her mother stepped back as if she'd been punched.

"You wanted my inheritance, you've got it. I hope it can bail you out of whatever mess you three have managed to get into," Amelia told her. "While you're treading water, I'll be serenely going about my life."

"You'll regret this Amelia and when she's done using you up like the paper napkin you are, don't come crawling back to me."

"I expect a stranger to wipe her boots on me, but you've been doing it most of my life," Amelia murmured. "I'd love to know why."

Felicia raked her with her gaze. "Your father left me with three children, refusing to pay any child support."

"That's not an excuse."

"His father insisted I sign a prenuptial agreement and he put me on an allowance," Felicia said.

"Let me guess, if he caught you cheating you forfeit whatever the agreement was for."

She shook her head. "He was such a jerk. I made one mistake, and he walked out on me, on you. He didn't even want you either." She laughed. "I just got stuck with you."

"I bet that surprised the hell out of you," Amelia muttered. "He couldn't be led around by the balls by a woman who couldn't keep her panties up."

Felicia sneered at her. "You're just like the bastard. Self-righteous, but what do you have? Nothing. Nothing! I have your inheritance, and I'm going to keep it."

"As soon as the door closes on you, I'll have peace of mind, my life, and contentment," she said. "More than you'll ever have because you'll always be a victim of your own greed."

Felicia looked down her nose at her. "Go ahead. Live in this backwoods town with that hick. See if I care. Just don't call me begging when she leaves you."

"I wouldn't dream of it, Mother, I'd rather spend the rest of my life alone in this town than listening to you belittle me."

Felicia gave her one last look and stalked from the room.

Amelia sighed and went into the bathroom to undress. She needed a shower to wash the taint of her old life off her for good.

Chapter Nineteen

After her shower, Amelia dressed in a simple dress and went to unpack her things. A lightness spread through her chest bringing a smile to her face.

Halfway finished, she went downstairs to make herself a cup of tea. The noise of her sister talking to her mother soon faded along with a close of the front door, and Amelia sipped her tea serenely.

The serenity faded with the sound of the car door slamming as her mind wandered to Ryan and the oddity of the hunger that had overtaken her.

Her gaze went to her hand where the crest was. It was visible now. What was wrong with her?

She had to know, and Amelia was certain it was more than just a sun allergy.

"Hello, Amelia."

She looked up, her aunt came into the room wearing a smile. "Did things go okay at your apartment?"

"Yes." She smiled. "Ryan was a big help. Aunt Genny, I want to talk to you about my father," Amelia said.

"Okay," she said and moved to the table, her expression hard to read. "I'll tell you what I can."

"Okay." She took a sip of her tea and waited. "I haven't seen any pictures of me and him. Who is he? Why are there no pictures of him? Why does my mother and grandmother despise him?"

"I can't answer those questions," she replied.

"What's his name?"

"His name is Novak Rose-Brier," Genny told her. "He's from a moderately wealthy family who lives out west. He used to live here."

"Why'd he go to the west?"

"His family had their reasons, but they do have a business there," she answered. "He was a good man. Kind, intelligent. He works for the family business. He creates perfume. He's remarried to a model. She was the face of the company's signature fragrance and one of their newer ones."

"Why didn't grandfather want him to marry her?"

"He thought it would be a disaster," she said quietly. "Novak is—was a quiet man. He and your mother were oil and water. She wanted to spend his inheritance, and he wouldn't allow it."

"Money."

"My father got together with the lawyers to strike up a compromise. Your father was to pay for your education, clothing and all of your educational needs including the summer camps, the summer abroad, and to provide you with the car you got after graduating high school."

She'd traded her car in after college.

"Your mother wasn't happy that she couldn't get her hands on your money. It was a sticking point in the divorce, but my father got them past it."

"Was leaving me part of the deal?"

"I don't know," she answered evenly. "I just know that after the divorce he moved out west."

"I'd like to meet him. Do you think you could contact him?"

"I'll hire a private detective," she said.

"Is he a vampire? Is that why I have a sun allergy?"

"Why would you ask that?" her aunt asked carefully.

"Because something strange is happening to me," Amelia answered. "I felt hungry, but I wasn't. My senses are sharper."

Her aunt sighed. "Your father is a vampire," she said quietly. "The amulet is to protect you against the sun."

The words were only marginally shocking, and Amelia closed her eyes for a moment allowing the words to sink in. "How long have you known?"

"I knew there was a chance you'd only carry the gene, but that's all it seemed. I never expected you to turn, but that you have doesn't change anything," Genny said.

Amelia sighed heavily as her brows drew into a frown.

How was she going to explain this to Ryan? Ryan would probably run from her one she learned she was a vampire who could kill her.

"I need more information," Amelia told her. "I need to know—why did he leave me if he knew?"

"You'll have to ask him, and I promise you I'll get him back here."

Amelia covered her mouth with her hand as she struggled to make sense of it all, to put thoughts into words.

"Your mother doesn't know, but—"

"Is this why you didn't want Ryan to go out with me? You were afraid I'd hurt her?"

Her aunt smiled faintly. "I was afraid she'd lead you on, and you'd get hurt. Ryan's a big girl, she can take care of her own feelings."

Amelia nodded. "But you know about my father because you're a vampire too." Amelia held her breath not sure what she wanted the answer to be.

"Yes." Genny shrugged. "I know you're upset—"

"I'm not upset," she broke in evenly. "I just need some time to think this all through, and I want one more night with Ryan before I have to break up with her." She got to her feet and hurried from the room.

She wouldn't be able to keep this a secret from Ryan too long. In any case, she wouldn't want to. Ryan deserved to know, and she wouldn't want her. Amelia understood.

She wasn't sure she'd want a monster either.

Chapter Twenty

Ryan smiled all the way home. Amelia wasn't the woman she expected to get involved with let alone be falling for. However, there was nothing about Amelia she didn't like, and Ryan wanted to get to know everything about her.

That she was one of them, would only make things easier in the long run. Course, they would have to talk soon, but Ryan wouldn't say anything until she'd talked to Miss Genny. She had a feeling Amelia had no idea about her heritage.

That was a shame, but it had probably been for the best with a mother like Amelia had.

Still, Amelia was obviously an energy vampire, something Ryan knew a little about. She didn't know the mechanics or how they came to be, but she'd met one in New York.

She had been a sensual delight when she wasn't working. The relationship hadn't lasted because the woman had been as into her work as Ryan had been. In the time they'd spent together, Ryan had learned how to feed an energy vampire.

Once she got home, Ryan sat down at her desk to do a little work on a file Ree had sent her. When she'd finished, she sent the file to Ree before taking a long leisurely shower. She dressed and grabbed some wine from her wine cellar to take to Amelia's. She headed for the front door and opened it to find Alston standing there.

"Mr. Alston," she said with a frown. "What are you doing here?"

"May I come in a moment, Ryan?" he asked.

"Sure." She motioned him in and closed the door.

"Wine. You must be going to see Amelia," he commented.

"I am in fact," she said. "I'll be late if we dawdle."

"I won't take up too much of your time. I just want to talk to you for a moment about Amelia."

"What about her, and what's it to you?" she asked patiently.

"You're feeding from her," he said without further preamble.

"Is that your business, Mr. Alston?" she asked coolly. "Or are you here under your Queen's orders to discuss it with me?"

"She's concerned about the situation, and she'd rather you allow her to tell Amelia about our world."

"I see," Ryan said tonelessly. "She wants me to lie to Amelia so she can be furious with me when she finds out I didn't tell her."

"If you haven't told her you're a vampire using her for a snack by now, I doubt you're going to rush to do it tonight."

Ryan studied him as she drew in a breath and slowly released it. "I don't like what you're implying," she said coldly. "I am not using her, and just for Miss Genny's information, Amelia—"

"She doesn't know, but she's curious about her amulet."

She laughed. "Is that what your coven calls it? It's a mark plain and simple."

"It protects us from the sun," he told her coldly.

"I know what it does," she answered.

Mihai had an amulet that protected him from the sun whenever he had to be out during the day, but it wasn't fused to his body.

"Just give me your word you'll allow us to talk to her before you say anything."

"Fine. Tell Miss Genny she has two weeks," she said.

"Amelia is part of the House of Thistle-Rose, and you have no right to claim any authority over her or dictate to our Queen."

"As she has none to dictate to me, Mr. Alston," she retorted. "I was under the impression you came here under friendly terms to make an informal request not give me orders."

He glared at her.

"You're an elder and that is the only reason I'm not kicking your ass out right now," she told him. "Also, I happen to like and respect you as a man."

"I—"

"I could rip your amulet off and toss your butt out into the sun or merely trap you in one of my rooms with a ward."

"You couldn't."

"Oh, I could," she told him calmly.

"You've never practiced with your mother's coven."

"As far as you know," she said. "But nothing proves I wasn't educated in her dark ways, and she did have some excellent wards against vampires even how to strip the protection from your amulet without ever taking it from your body. Would you like me to demonstrate?"

Fear crossed his face, and he glanced around.

"There is no direct sunlight into this space out of consideration for Mihai," she told him with a smile.

The foyer of her home had no windows, a design flaw she'd been told when she'd bought the house. It had belonged to an old vampire who'd been killed by her father. She'd inherited the house when she'd turned sixteen, but the man she called her dad hadn't known.

He didn't know a great deal about her life. Mihai had been educating and training her since she was twelve. Her father had wanted her groomed to take over the House of Knight and that had included ensuring that she sired no less than sixteen people by her thirtieth birthday.

At thirty, she was meant to join the house as an elder before becoming its primary leader. In preparation, her mother had also introduced her to magic that could protect her against other vampires as well as command, control, and destroy them.

They were secrets her father, who'd been a sorcerer, had sought. It was the reason he'd come here. He'd wanted the grimoire of an old Cajun voodoo priestess. That had been Ryan's grandmother. Her mother had inherited the family book of secret and dark magic. She knew Mihai had wanted the book, but like her father, he'd been unable to find it. Not even the coven knew where the book was.

Only one person did know where her family legacy of magic was hidden.

"Ryan—"

"Good evening Mr. Alston," she said.

"I want your word."

"I gave you all that I'm going to," she replied. "I'll say nothing for two weeks."

"Is that your word?"

"Yes."

"Thank you." He gave her a nod and moved for the door, stopping. "There was a rumor your mother possessed a book of old and dark magic." He faced her then. His gaze assessing her.

"I've heard that too."

"Does her coven have it?"

"I wouldn't know," she answered. "I was still young when my mother died, Mr. Alston. She didn't speak of such things to me or in my hearing."

"Right. She was a classy lady." He inclined his head and exited her home.

Ryan smiled as she followed in his wake. Did anyone seriously think she'd tell them about that book?

Ryan climbed into her truck and put the bottle on the passenger seat and started the engine. That book would one day become a serious bone of contention between her and other vampires, but her mother had armed her well with the knowledge she'd destroy them with if they forced her hand.

Her drive to the Honeywell home was a quick one, but Ryan noticed someone following her at a discreet distance. She dismissed it but made note of the car that turned off before she reached the house.

She was about to take over one of the most prestigious houses in the south. However, Ryan hadn't expected it to come with any real problems. She could be wrong.

Ryan pulled into the driveway of the home with a smile. She was looking forward to spending more time with Amelia. She was certain they had the makings of something special.

She rang the bell, and Amelia opened the door to her, and Ryan smiled. "Hi, Amelia." Her gaze slid over the other woman who was clad in a simple dress, hair flowing over her shoulders.

"You look beautiful."

"Thanks," she said. "Come in. I've set things up. My Aunt Genny is in her bedroom watching TV. We can't use the guest house until next week. Aunt Genny is having some work done on it."

"That's okay."

Amelia took her hand. "I made coffee and cake."

"I love cake," Ryan said.

"Good." Amelia gave her a shy smile and led her through the house to a small sitting room. The room's lights were dimmed, and a blanket was spread out with candles lighting the room. Soft music played.

"This is fantastic. You didn't have to go to so much trouble."

"I have a lot of lost time to make up for," Amelia told her. "So, may I have this dance?"

"My pleasure," Ryan said, and Amelia led her to the area designated for dancing.

Ryan took Amelia in her arms, and they swayed to the slow ballad. They danced twice more before sitting down to dessert. Amelia served her, and Ryan tasted the cake.

"You made this?" Ryan asked.

"No. I didn't have time." Amelia smiled. "Plus, I was tired after the drive."

"How are you handling all this?" Ryan asked.

Amelia shrugged. "If by this you mean my family not speaking to me anymore, fine. I think I always knew it was going to come to this."

"What are you going to do now?" Ryan asked.

"Live." She shrugged. There was a hint of sadness in her voice that had Ryan frowning.

"What's wrong, Amelia? You can tell me."

Amelia gave her a smile. "I want a real relationship with you, Ryan."

"But?"

"But nothing," she said softly, shaking her head sending tendrils of red hair dancing around her face.

Ryan reached out and tugged a strand of her hair. "I think we both know we're already on the road to something." She wasn't sure what, but her heart clearly already wanted Amelia.

Ryan wasn't inclined to walk away from a woman that could be the one.

"You're good for me Ryan Baptist," she whispered.

Ryan gave her a wink. "I think we're good for each other." She finished her cake and took up her cup to take a sip of the rich brew.

They were a good match, but time would tell if they were perfect together.

Chapter Twenty-One

In her office, Genny sat behind her desk finalizing some plans. She wanted everything in place before she left and that meant she'd begin Amelia's indoctrination into the coven as soon as tomorrow.

She wouldn't inundate her with the information, but she would start her education to make the transition smoother. And if Amelia couldn't accept who she was, she'd have to allow the elders to take full control of the coven until she returned.

She would also have to contact Novak, but that she would do by phone rather than in an email.

Her phone rang as she closed the file on her computer and Genny picked it up and glanced at the display. "Hello Felicia," she said coolly. "Did you make it back home okay?"

"Fine," she said. "I want my half of the property. I want you to sell it."

Genny sighed heavily. "Felicia, I know your mother had no idea or she probably never even thought about it, but you don't have a half for me to give you."

"What are you talking about?" she demanded. "Dad left me half of everything."

"He couldn't leave you what didn't belong to him."

"What are you talking about?" Felicia demanded. "The inn with it's extensive property belonged to him along with a little cabin there."

"It belonged to my mother," Genny told her with a smile. She would finally be able to cut her ties with her half-sister and her stepmother.

"That—"

"Is true," she cut in quickly. "Felicia, the property belonged to my mother and came to me on her death. My father was just the executor. Course, things were set up so that if anything happened to me, you and your children inherited my estate."

"I don't believe you," she said.

"That doesn't really matter," Genny answered. "What does is you and your mother have no jurisdiction over the inn. It's all mine."

"I'll have my lawyer contact you."

"No, your lawyer can contact mine. All of the papers are in order. Goodbye Felicia." She ended the call with a smile.

Her sister would look into things and find that she had no claim on the property especially with her alive. She hadn't changed her will leaving Amelia everything yet, just the controlling interest in the inn, but she'd take care of that as soon as Amelia claimed her birthright.

Genny glanced out of the window and saw Amelia and Ryan in the garden. They were kissing. She could tell just by looking at them together, they had the same thing she had with Alston. Or they were at the beginning of that enduring love that would see them each through any challenge that came.

The End

Coming Soon
Winter's Kiss
Gray Light Rises

More by Serenity Snow

Assassin's Core Series

Fairy Mafia Series

Windswept Series

Coyote Bound Series

Law and Love Series

Submitting to the Hellhound

Sensation, Louisiana Series

Assassins Trilogy

Find me on the web: Spice of Life Romance - Serenity Snow Romances (weebly.com)[1]

---

1. https://spiceofliferomance.weebly.com/

Don't miss out!

Visit the website below and you can sign up to receive emails whenever Serenity Snow publishes a new book. There's no charge and no obligation.

https://books2read.com/r/B-A-JTRI-CJCFC

About the Author

Serenity Snow is a voracious reader of romances and loves a happy ending. Serenity thinks fall is the perfect time of year for romance because the weather is still warm enough for walks in the park and pretty enough to create a romantic atmosphere for outdoor dining.

Serenity writes sensual lesbian romance of the paranromal and shifter variety.

Read more at https://spiceofliferomance.weebly.com/.